MAYA
The Accidental Spy

ANJU SINGH

INDIA • SINGAPORE • MALAYSIA

Copyright © Anju Singh 2025
All rights reserved.

ISBN
Paperback 979-8-89724-984-8
Hardcase 979-8-89906-967-3

This book has been published with all efforts taken to make the material error-free after the consent of the author. However, the author and the publisher do not assume and hereby disclaim any liability to any party for any loss, damage, or disruption caused by errors or omissions, whether such errors or omissions result from negligence, accident, or any other cause.

While every effort has been made to avoid any mistake or omission, this publication is being sold on the condition and understanding that neither the author nor the publishers or printers would be liable in any manner to any person by reason of any mistake or omission in this publication or for any action taken or omitted to be taken or advice rendered or accepted on the basis of this work. For any defect in printing or binding the publishers will be liable only to replace the defective copy by another copy of this work then available.

Disclaimer

This is a work of fiction. Any resemblance to real events, persons, or places is purely coincidental. The story, including its characters, incidents, and references to political topics is entirely a product of the author's imagination. It does not depict real-life occurrences and has no basis in reality.

Acknowledgment

Writing a book is a journey, and I feel incredibly grateful for the love and support that made this one possible.

First and foremost, my Mom Mrs. Sudha Singh, my biggest cheerleader, my constant believer. No matter how small or big my success was, you were always the first to celebrate it. I miss you every single day, but I know you're watching over me, probably rolling your eyes at my late-night writing habits but still proud. Miss you, Mumma. This one's for you.

To my husband, Ayush Nirwan—my personal nighttime therapist and head massage expert. Since my creativity conveniently wakes up after 11 PM, you've been there, half-asleep, rubbing my head after every chapter because, of course, with great imagination comes a great headache! I don't know if you signed up for this, but hey, no refunds now. Thanks for being my rock (and my pain relief).

And a huge thanks to my friend, Vishwa Vivek, for being the first and only reader of my drafts, giving me honest feedback, and making sure I didn't go off the rails with my storytelling. While everyone else was unbothered when I sent my drafts for feedback, he actually read them (yes, all of them!) and gave me genuine, unbiased opinions. Every writer needs that one friend who says, "Yeah… maybe not this part," and he did it with brutal honesty and a great sense of humor.

This book is not just my work—it carries pieces of the love, patience, and encouragement I received along the way. A heartfelt Thank you to you all!

With gratitude,
Anju Singh

Contents

Chapter 1

The Dental Appointment

I t was raining, creating a beautiful but gloomy landscape outside. Maya sat by the window, sipping a cup of tea while watching the view. Her roommate, Smriti, called her from behind.

"Maya!"

Maya didn't turn around. "Yes, what happened?"

Smriti approached, wiping tears from her eyes. "That swine yelled at me again."

Maya looked at her, her big brown eyes wide with curiosity, but she smiled. "Now what?"

Smriti sniffled, clearly upset. "He promised he'd call as soon as he landed in India, but it's been almost four hours, and he hasn't even said 'hi' to me. So when I called, he yelled at me, saying he was with his family, and then he just disconnected the call."

Maya and Smriti were flat mates living in Canada. Maya worked at a software company, while Smriti worked at Costco in sales.

Maya leaned back in her chair, unbothered. "So what's wrong? You know he's been away for three years and now he's finally spending time with his family. I'm sure he's not missing you much. You need to understand that."

With a teasing smile, she got up and headed toward the kitchen. Smriti, already irritated, stormed off to her room. "You're not helping, Maya!"

The next morning, Maya was working from home when a reminder popped up on her screen: Dental Cleaning Appointment.

"Oh, No! I almost forgot," Maya muttered. Getting a dental appointment in Canada was difficult, so she quickly called her colleague, Tanay. "Can you handle my tasks for the next three hours? I can't miss this appointment."

After parking the car at the clinic, Maya noticed a quote written on the car next to hers: "A soulmate doesn't necessarily mean a partner."

Maya stared at it. "What rubbish. It doesn't even make sense," she said to herself.

She entered the clinic and rushed to the reception, where a woman was sitting. "Hi, my name is Maya Sharma. I have an appointment with Dr. Vishesh Khurana."

Before the receptionist could check, they both heard laughter behind them. Dr. Vishesh was talking to an older man, who was praising him.

"You should be a philosopher, not a dentist," the old man said, laughing. "You have wisdom, Vishesh. May you always keep spreading that."

Vishesh laughed, nodding. "Thanks, Tom. And remember, life's days are limited, just like our teeth, so let's show them off as much as we can," he added, winking.

Maya raised an eyebrow, thinking, what just happened? This is so cheesy.

Vishesh caught her gaze and smiled before turning to the receptionist. "Hey, Dona, any more appointments for today?"

Dona checked her schedule. "Well, this lady was scheduled for 12:15 p.m., but it's already 12:40."

"Hm," Vishesh said, glancing back at Maya. "Send her in."

Dona hesitated. "But it's your lunch break, Dr. Vishesh."

Vishesh ignored her, smiling at Maya. "Hi, I'm Dr. Vishesh." He extended his hand.

Maya hesitated but shook his hand.

Dona chuckled as Vishesh turned to her. "Look at her Dona isn't she beautiful? I can give up one lunch just to see her smile."

Maya rolled her eyes, her expression flat, and Vishesh immediately realized his attempt to flirt had failed. "Okay, let's go to the cabin," he said, trying to get the procedure started.

As Maya sat in the dental chair, she thought, what kind of cheesy man is this? Seems like a huge Shah Rukh Khan fan, full of Hindi movie clichés.

Meanwhile, Vishesh was preparing for the procedure, glancing at Maya. Is she depressed or something? I cracked a joke, but she didn't even smile. Maybe she's one of those who think the world revolves around her beauty. I'm a dentist, and making people smile is my job. Typical Karen from Hollywood, huh?

"Could you please open your mouth?" Vishesh asked, beginning the cleaning procedure.

As he worked, he hummed a song. Maya tried to recall it, it was one of her favorite songs. She closed her eyes, concentrating, but Vishesh misinterpreted her silence.

"You seem very sensitive," he remarked. "I'm just using water to clean the plaque, you know."

Maya opened her eyes and shot him an irritated look, rolling her eyes. Vishesh murmured to himself, "Typical Karen vibes."

After about 45 minutes, the procedure was finished. Vishesh handed her a slip with the stamp and date so she could submit it for insurance reimbursement. "You can collect the invoice from Dona. You might feel some sensitivity to cold or hot food or drinks; if it happens, come back again, Ms...?"

"Maya. Maya Sharma."

When Vishesh heard her name, something clicked in his mind. He had a flashback to his college days, sitting with friends, playing truth or dare.

"Truth or dare?" one of his friends asked.

"Truth," he replied.

"Tell us about your girlfriend," a girl named Pooja pressed.

"I don't have one," he answered nonchalantly.

"No way! You're lying," Pooja said, laughing. "You must be waiting for a fairy from heaven."

The group teased him, and one of the boys mockingly added, "Yeah, and her name will be Mohini!"

Vishesh dramatically turned to the group, "No, Mohini's too basic. Her name will be Maya," he said, making the declaration with flair.

Back in the present, Vishesh saw Maya rushing out of the clinic. He quickly turned to Dona, who told him, "She already left. She got a call from her office and said she'd come back tomorrow to collect her invoice. She also left her health card here."

Vishesh stood there for a moment, a bit lost in thought. The name Maya had triggered something from the past, but now, it seemed like fate was playing its part.

Chapter 2

The Gas Station

Smriti entered the flat, flicked on the light, and scanned the room. Maya was still on a conference call.

"You're still working? It's 8:30 PM!" Smriti whispered, her voice carrying a mix of surprise and disbelief.

Maya barely looked up, nodding with a strained expression that suggested she was long past the point of enjoying her job. She mumbled something in agreement, her eyes glued to the screen.

Smriti, already heading to her room, muttered a half-hearted, "Okay then," and shut the door behind her.

Almost 20 minutes later, just as Smriti was about to scroll through her phone, the sound of Maya's phone ringing broke the silence. It was Dona from the dental clinic.

"Hey, Maya, it's Dona. Just calling to remind you about your outstanding payment, and also, when will you be picking up your health card?" the voice on the other end asked.

"Ah, sorry, Dona, I was caught up today. Could you email me the invoice? I'll pay it right away. Thanks!" Maya replied quickly, trying to get back to her work.

A few minutes later, Maya knocked on Smriti's door, her face full of exhaustion.

"Hey, could you do me a favor?" Maya asked, pushing the door open slightly. "I have to head to the Mississauga office tomorrow for a team meeting. The new CEO is coming in, and I need to be there."

Smriti, half-focused on her Instagram feed, raised an eyebrow. "And you need me to help you with what exactly?"

Maya sighed. "Could you visit the Smile Dental Clinic and pick up my health card? I'm too swamped."

Smriti mockingly raised her eyebrows, remembering something from the day before. "Remember how you laughed at me yesterday when I came to you about my boyfriend yelling at me? Well, now you need my help."

Maya rolled her eyes, clearly too tired for the banter. "Oh, come on, Sim! You know you were overreacting. Please, I'm begging you."

Smriti put her phone down, feigning reluctance. "Alright, alright, fine. WhatsApp me the address, and I'll go tomorrow."

Meanwhile, Vishesh's flat was near the elevator. As he struggled with his keys, the door to the lift opened, and Mr. Saroha stepped out.

"Ah, Vishesh! How are you, young man? It's been so long!" Mr. Saroha said, pulling Vishesh into a hug.

Vishesh smiled and replied, "Yes, I'm a smile specialist. If I'm not busy, that means people aren't smiling enough!"

Mr. Saroha burst out laughing. "I like your humor, man. We should sit down for drinks sometime it's been 2 months since you shifted here and have not yet been to my apartment!"

"Sure, sir," Vishesh responded, amused.

As Vishesh opened his flat door, his phone rang- He picked it up, listened intently for a moment, then responded.

"Yes, I'm settled here," he said softly.

The next morning, Smriti entered the Smile Dental Clinic.

"Hi, I'm here to collect the health card for Ms. Maya Sharma," she said to the receptionist.

At that moment, Vishesh walked into the clinic. He noticed Smriti standing there and couldn't resist walking over.

"Hi, do you know Maya?" Vishesh asked casually.

"Yeah, she's my flat mate," Smriti replied, a bit distracted.

Vishesh grinned. "Is she the type who never smiles?"

Smriti laughed, shaking her head. "Oh, she smiles, but not much. She's just... like that."

Vishesh chuckled. "Well, no offense. I was just curious. Anyway, have a good one!" He turned to head toward his office.

As Smriti walked back to her car, her phone rang.

"Hey, Mimi!" Maya's voice sounded irritated.

Smriti laughed. "Oh, shut up, Sim! You know I hate it when you call me that!"

Maya grumbled, "Did you get my card?"

Smriti smirked. "Yes, found your card—and an admirer too."

"Admirer?" Maya's voice shifted to surprise. "Who?"

"Dr. Vishesh," Smriti teased. "He was asking about you. He wanted to know why you don't smile much."

Maya scoffed, "I do smile, just not at stupid jokes."

Smriti chuckled. "I told him you don't smile much."

Maya huffed. "Yeah, yeah, good for you," she muttered before disconnecting the call.

It was almost 9 PM, and Maya was driving home. She had a long stretch of road ahead, about 100 kilometers from her house. As she neared the final stretch, the fuel meter flickered, warning her that she was running low on gas. She was just 15 minutes away from home when the car sputtered to a stop.

She pulled into the nearest gas station; grateful it was still open. After filling up, she walked toward the convenience store to grab a coffee. But as she moved toward the store, she noticed a group of four or five junkies sitting nearby. They were watching her with unsettling stares. Trying to ignore them, she entered the store and grabbed her coffee.

When she stepped back outside, her heart raced. The junkies had spread out across the parking lot. Two of them were near her car, eyeing her purse.

Fear shot through her. She quickly decided to walk to the other side of the lot, hoping to get enough space and time to call for help. Behind the convenience store was a cannabis dispensary, (a store selling drugs) and as she turned the corner, she spotted a car with a quote on its back mirror: "A soulmate doesn't necessarily mean a partner."

She knew that car. The realization brought a wave of relief.

It might be Vishesh's car.

Maya stepped back behind the car, hoping to stay out of sight while she called 911. At the same moment, Vishesh came out of the dispensary and saw her hiding behind his vehicle.

"Maya?" he asked, confused but concerned.

"Some junkies are near my car," she explained nervously. "I'm just calling for help."

Vishesh didn't hesitate. "Don't call 911, they will ask unnecessary questions just take my car," he said, handing her his keys. "Go, and give me yours."

Maya didn't question it. She got into his car and drove off quickly, her eyes darting nervously as she reversed out of the spot. As she drove away, Vishesh stood in the parking lot, watching her leave.

"You're welcome," he shouted, shaking his head," No Thank you" he murmured to himself huh?

Later that night, Smriti was jolted awake by the sound of the doorbell ringing incessantly.

She rushed to the door, surprised to see Maya standing there, breathless and shaken.

"Maya, what happened?" Smriti asked, pulling her inside.

Maya recounted the entire story, her voice trembling a little. Smriti handed her a glass of water.

"Did you thank Dr Vishesh?" Smriti asked, raising an eyebrow.

Maya took a sip and glanced at her, almost embarrassed. "No... I was scared, and I rushed out. But I'll visit the clinic tomorrow and thank him, and return his car."

Smriti smiled, clearly relieved. "Good girl."

Chapter 3

A Table for Two

Maya woke up to the sound of her phone's alarm. Groggily, she squinted at the time—it was 6:45 AM. She groaned, realizing it was Saturday. Without much thought, she snuggled deeper into her blanket. But then, sleep eluded her as the memories of the previous night flooded back.

She had been in a rush when she left the office, and the thought that she should have checked her fuel tank nagged at her. Then, she recalled him—Dr. Vishesh. What was he doing outside the cannabis store? She had a thousand questions, and they kept circling in her mind. Should she just hand the car keys to Dona and avoid meeting him? But, would that be rude? After all, he had helped her at the right moment when she needed it most.

Still, his flirtatious smile lingered in her mind. She remembered the first time they met at the clinic. "I could give up one lunch to make her smile," he had said, his voice light with teasing. Maya shook her head, trying to shake off the confusion. But the thoughts kept spiraling.

She checked the time again. It was already 7:45 AM. With a sigh, she stood up, tying her hair loosely, and heading for the bathroom.

At 9 AM, Smriti walked out of her room, yawning.

"Morning, Mimi. You're up early," she said, noticing Maya sipping her coffee.

Maya gave her a side-eye before taking another sip.

"What's up? You look like you had the weirdest dream," Smriti teased, still half asleep.

Maya hesitated, clearly troubled. "Sim, I need your help."

Smriti blinked. "Uh-oh, okay, shoot."

Maya looked at her friend. "Dr. Vishesh... He was outside the cannabis store last night."

Smriti raised an eyebrow. "So?"

"I don't know, Sim. He's a dentist! What was he doing there? Is he... one of those people?"

Smriti burst out laughing. "What? He's a dentist, not a saint. Let the man live a little."

"I just don't know if I should see him again. I don't want to make it weird," Maya admitted.

"Girl, just thank him and return the keys. Don't overthink it." Smriti waved her hand dismissively. "You're making this more complicated than it needs to be."

Maya sighed. "But it's not just that. I'm not sure how to handle this. Should I just go meet him, thank him, and leave? Maybe I'll get Dona to handle it."

Smriti laughed. "Maya, you're being dramatic. Just go. You owe him a thank you, and you're holding his keys."

After some back-and-forth, Maya decided to call Dona to arrange the exchange. Dona wasn't at the clinic, but she told Maya to head there anyway. Maya reluctantly agreed, figuring she'd just keep it short and simple.

On her way to the clinic, Maya saw her blue Mazda waiting at a red light she looked closely it was Dr. Vishesh driving the car. He was turning the other way, so she quickly parked her car at the nearest parking and called Dona again.

"Hey, Dona. Is there any chance I could get Dr. Vishesh's number?"

Dona agreed, and moments later, Maya found herself staring at the screen, debating whether to call him or not. Finally, she decided to send a text.

Maya: Hi, it's Maya.

Vishesh: Hi, Maya! I was planning to return your car, but since Dona's on leave, I couldn't get your number.

Maya: I was actually on my way to the clinic. Are you still there?

Vishesh: Oh, I left early, but if you're still in need of the car, I am going to The Golden Froth Cafe. I'll be there in 15 minutes.

Maya typed "No" and deleted it four times before finally sending an "OK."

When Maya arrived at the café, she saw Vishesh waiting by the reception, his head buried in his phone. He suddenly looked up and saw Maya walking toward him, her presence somehow commanding the space around her. She wasn't too tall, nor too short—exactly 5 feet 5 inches, standing with an easy confidence. She wore blue bootcut jeans that hugged her frame just right, paired with a simple white cotton shirt. The sleeves of the shirt were casually rolled up, revealing a golden watch on her left wrist and a delicate, thin bracelet of the same metal on her right hand. Her hair, shoulder-length and soft, framed her face, the natural waves bouncing lightly with each step. She wore her sunglasses pushed up on her head as if they were more of a hair accessory than eyewear. Her skin, flawless and fair, glowed with a sun-kissed warmth, the faint pink of her cheeks a sign she had been outside. Her makeup was minimal, just enough to accentuate her striking features— natural, effortless beauty.

As she walked in, their eyes met, and for a brief moment, she could see the smile playing on his lips.

She approached him, a little nervous, holding the keys.

"Hi, Vishesh," she said, her voice low.

He smiled up at her. "Hey, Maya."

Kevin, the barista, greeted them with a playful smile. "Table for two, huh?"

Vishesh chuckled nervously, and Maya didn't even acknowledge Kevin's comment as she looked down at her phone. The exchange of keys felt awkward.

"Thank you for helping me last night," Maya murmured. She slid the keys across the table.

Vishesh waved her thanks away. "It was nothing. But you should stay. The hazelnut coffee with almond milk here is a must-try."

Maya hesitated. "No, I'm fine. I should get going."

But as she stood up to leave, her handbag accidentally hit an old man sitting at the table next to theirs.

"Sorry," she apologized quickly, but the old man scowled, muttering under his breath.

"These Indians, everywhere. I don't know why the government allows them here," he grumbled.

Vishesh watched as Maya's expression shifted from mild discomfort to a quiet, simmering anger. She turned toward the old man, her voice still composed but now laced with steel. "Hello, sir," she said, her tone measured, "why are you being so mean? I apologized, didn't I?"

The old man sneered, his gaze dismissive. "Your cute voice can't make me like you, so cut it."

That was the moment Maya snapped. Without warning, she pushed back from the table, her eyes burning with something fierce, and walked straight over to the old man. She sat down across from him, her finger jabbing the air as she spoke. "Look, Mr. Whatever you are," she began, her voice steady but full of authority, "I don't know what went wrong in your life today. Maybe your dog died, or your third wife is asking for a divorce. Or maybe your teenage granddaughter just told you she's pregnant. Whatever it is, it's not my problem. I made a mistake, I apologized, and that's all there is to it."

She stood up then, her body suddenly straight and proud, like a warrior preparing for battle. "And don't you ever speak a word against my country again, Just because I'm sitting in your country doesn't mean I hate mine, okay?"

With one final, defiant glance, she turned on her heel, her posture still radiating strength as she marched back to the table, leaving the old man stunned and speechless. Vishesh, who had been watching the exchange with wide eyes, couldn't help but admire the raw power in her response. He'd never seen anyone stand their ground quite like that.

"Wow," he said softly, a grin tugging at the corner of his lips.

Maya sat down, slightly embarrassed but not sorry. "I don't know what came over me".

Kevin appeared at the table, breaking the tension. "Ready to order yet?"

Maya, still flustered, smiled awkwardly. "Yes, I'll have the hazelnut coffee with almond milk."

Vishesh laughed softly, shaking his head. "I see what's happening here... it's your favorite coffee now, not because I suggested it, right?"

Maya blushed but managed a smile. "Sorry, I didn't mean to make it sound like that. It's just... I can't tolerate people disrespecting my country."

Vishesh nodded. "You did the right thing. But let me ask you something... if you love India so much, why are you living in Canada?"

Maya took a deep breath, looking out the window. "It's fate. It just... happened."

As they sipped their coffees, a comfortable silence settled between them. Maya couldn't help but think of why was Vishesh coming out of the cannabis store.

"By the way," she asked, suddenly shy. "What were you doing... aaa,

what perfume were you wearing last night? It was... nice." she changed her question.

Vishesh's eyes sparkled with mischief. "Oh, I was coming out of a cannabis store. I probably smelled like weed."

Maya's eyes widened, and she looked down, embarrassed.

"I was getting something for an elderly man he lives in my building. He loves to vape," Vishesh explained. "I'm not into that stuff, though."

Maya finally smiled. "Thanks again, Vishesh. I should go now."

He stood up as she did. "But let me pay for the coffee please just as a Thank you" Maya insisted.

Vishesh smiled back. "Okay, next time it's on me".

Vishesh watched Maya as she turned away, her face still flushed with the remnants of her fiery exchange. There was something about her—her confidence, the way she carried herself, the sharpness in her eyes that dared anyone to challenge her. What a beautiful face, he thought, a smile tugging at the corners of his lips. Her smile... topped with that attitude...

The thought lingered, surprising him as it settled in his chest. Am I in love with Maya Sharma?

He chuckled quietly to himself, unsure if the flutter in his stomach was from admiration or something else entirely. But whatever it was, it felt new, and it felt real. And for the first time in a long while, he wasn't sure what to make of it.

Chapter 4

Maya's Mind, Unfolding in Ink

As Maya left, Vishesh's phone rang. He quickly takes the call. The voice on the other end was low, Vishesh nodded, his face unreadable. "On my way," he replied, his voice steady but urgent.

Moments later, Vishesh pulled into his building's parking lot. He spotted Mr. Saroha leaving, waiting for his car to exit the society gates. As soon as Mr. Saroha's vehicle passed through, Vishesh swiftly got out of his own car and headed toward the 5th-floor, apartment—number 505, Mr. Saroha's residence. He pressed the doorbell, his fingers tapping anxiously on his jacket sleeve.

Mrs. Saroha answered the door. "Yes?" she asked, her expression neutral.

Vishesh chuckled, flashing a polite smile. "Oh, hi, Mrs. Saroha! Is Mr. Saroha around? I'm Dr. Vishesh, I live just down the hall in apartment 502. I wanted to speak with him."

As he spoke, Vishesh tried to glance inside, attempting to catch a glimpse of the apartment's interior, but Mrs. Saroha didn't open the door wide enough for him to see much. Her response was curt, her tone cool. "He's not home, he went to India for a few days."

Vishesh smiled politely, masking the flicker of disappointment. "No issues, nothing urgent. I'll be back when Mr. Saroha is back " He nodded and turned to leave.

Back at his car, Vishesh was about to grab his briefcase when he noticed the charging cable had fallen under the passenger seat. As he leaned down to pick it up, something else caught his eye—a small leather-bound diary tucked beneath the seat. His fingers brushed against it, and with a frown, he picked it up. "This might be Maya's," he murmured to himself.

Maya opened the door to find Smriti lounging on the couch, eyes glued to the TV. "Hi," Maya said, holding up the bags of food. "I brought us dinner."

Smriti's head snapped up, her nose immediately twitching as she caught the aroma. She bolted off the couch and hurried over to Maya, eagerly ripping open one of the packets.

"Wait, wait," Maya said, laughing. "Let me change first."

Smriti shot her a teasing grin. "Take your time. I've got plenty of time to hear all the juicy details about your meeting with Dr. Vishesh."

Maya responded "What details? with a half-smile. It was just a short meeting. Straight to the point. Nothing much."

Smriti gave her a mockingly irritated look. "You're so boring, Maya. You've got to tell me something."

Maya chuckled, shaking her head. "Seriously, we just had coffee. That's it."

Smriti raised an eyebrow. "Nothing else?" she asked, a little too loudly, sounding both surprised and disappointed.

Maya shrugged, trying to keep it casual. "Well, you know, you were right this morning. I was being a little dramatic. I judged him based on our first meeting at the clinic. He seemed a little... flirtatious then. And then I ran into him at that cannabis store. Everything just felt off. But—"

Smriti's eyes widened in anticipation. "But?"

Maya grinned, leaning against the doorframe. "But today, he was nice. No flirting. In fact, I might have caused a little scene, and he appreciated me for what I did."

Smriti's face lit up. "Aww! So when's the next date?"

Maya rolled her eyes. "No date is happening here," she muttered, walking away as Smriti's delighted laughter echoed behind her.

Visheh couldn't resist so he started reading Maya's diary: on the front page it was beautifully written "Maya's mind, unfolding in ink". Vishesh smiled a little as he turned to the next page

22 December 2016
(It was a poem)
Be It

The world will come with hands outstretched,
A smile so sweet, yet plans engraved cold,
They'll take, they'll use, then walk away,
When they've had their fill, when they've had their say.

They'll leave behind their empty trace,
Their love a mask, their hearts a chase,
And in the silence, I'll be left,
With the rawest truth, and the heart is heft.

But be it. I will give it again,
Even knowing how this ends.

When the world has turned its back,
I will always have my heart intact.

So let them leave, let them forget,
I'll love again, and not regret.
For in the end, when all is done,
I'll be with me, the only one.

And be it, I'll do it all once more,
A heart that loves, forever pure.
For, in the end, it's all I need—
To stand with myself, my soul freed.

While reading the poem, Vishesh murmured to himself, "Hmm... who dared to break Maya's heart?" The words lingered in his mind as he turned the page, his fingers grazing over the smooth paper. As he flipped through, he noticed some pages were torn—ripped out, perhaps in haste, as if something had been erased, forgotten, or lost.

He moved forward, his eyes scanning the next entry, dated 30th March 2018.

"I saw him today, happy and stress-free with some other girl. He got engaged, I heard. She was looking beautiful. I don't know why, but it pains me. Why am I not as happy as he is? This question haunts me every night. I can spend the day working, giving my 100% at work, but why can't I sleep?"

Vishesh lingered on the words, feeling the weight of her sadness before he turned the page again, unable to stop himself from reading on. It felt too personal, too raw, but he couldn't look away.

The next entry was dated 5ᵗʰ February 2022.

"I wish I was there with Mom during her last breath. I wanted to talk to her, but why was she taken? She was not ill... She must have had something to tell me. I had a lot to share. Why did I go on that trip? I should have said no. At least I would have had three more days to talk to her. I know, Mom, I was rude to you at times, but trust me, I love you the most."

The words blurred towards the end as if a tear had dropped on the paper, smudging the ink. Vishesh paused, his chest tightening, a sense of quiet reverence filling the air. He closed the diary gently.

Vishesh picked his phone opened WhatsApp and searched for Maya's number and typed-

Hi Maya! and he was eagerly waiting for her response, almost after 5 minutes she responded "Hello".

Vishesh was excited to see her message "I just wanted to ask if you are, ok?"

Maya saw the text and replied in surprise "Ya I am ok, why?"

Vishesh- Nothing just asking.

Maya- All good here, Thanks.

Vishesh was struggling to think what to ask her next as he was feeling an all different level of connection and wanted her to talk to him.

Maya's response broke the chain of his thoughts "Ok good night".

Vishesh was disappointed and replied "Good night".

The next morning was pleasant, and the quiet of the society park wrapped around Vishesh like a welcome cloak. He sat on one of the benches, letting the stillness of the day clear until a voice from the gate caught his attention. A delivery man stood there, asking the security guard for the buzzer code to the building. Vishesh watched as the guard inquired about the apartment number.

"Mrs. Saroha's," the delivery guy answered without hesitation.

The guard tapped his access card, granting him entry. Vishesh's pulse quickened. He stood up and, without a second thought, began walking toward the gate. He had to follow. As the delivery man entered the building, Vishesh slipped behind him, matching his pace. They approached the elevator together, and Vishesh struck up a casual conversation.

"Busy with morning deliveries?" Vishesh asked.

The delivery guy nodded. "Yes, sir. Lots of orders today."

The man had pressed the button for the fifth floor. An idea sparked in Vishesh's mind.

"Oh, I saw you pressed for the fifth floor," he said, trying to sound casual. "Which apartment are you going to?"

"505," the delivery guy replied.

Vishesh's heart raced. This could be the break he'd been waiting for. A chance to get a closer look into Mr. Saroha's flat.

He seized the moment. "Actually, I am friends with Mr. Saroha and I live on the same floor as he does. I can take the groceries up for you if you'd like. It'll save you some time."

At first, the delivery guy hesitated, shaking his head. "Sorry, I can't hand over the groceries to you." But just as he spoke, his phone buzzed in his pocket. He pulled it out, reading the message from the next scheduled delivery that flashed across the screen—When are you coming? I need the delivery soon.

"Well, the order is prepaid so alright," the man said, a reluctant smile tugging at his lips. "Just make sure you ask Mr.Saroha to send me the code in the app so that I can mark the delivery status as done ."

"Done", Vishesh replied.

Vishesh's hand trembled slightly as he rang the doorbell. Moments later, the door creaked open, revealing Mr. Saroha's house help, a middle-aged woman with a tired expression. She looked him up and down, then asked flatly, "Yes?"

Vishesh cleared his throat, trying to sound calm. "Is Mrs. Saroha home?"

The woman gave a small shake of her head. "She's sleeping."

He hesitated, then added, "I'm here to deliver the groceries. The bags are pretty heavy. Could you please let me in?"

The lady sighed but stepped aside, allowing him to enter. Just as he entered, a voice called from the other room. A young man, somewhere in his late twenties, appeared in the hallway. His gaze flickered briefly from the lady to Vishesh.

"Who's this?" the man asked, his tone sharp.

The lady answered without much emotion. "He's here to deliver the groceries."

The man looked at Vishesh, his expression a mix of confusion and suspicion. "Is this already paid for?" he asked.

Vishesh's heart raced, but he kept his smile in place. "Let me check," He fumbled with his phone, pretending to text someone. In the blink of an eye, his camera snapped a picture of the man. He looked up, and said "Actually, I'm not the delivery guy. I'm your neighbor. I just happened to be coming to the same floor. I have texted the delivery guy, and he'll call you if it's not paid. I only came in to offer help."

The man's face hardened, his eyes cold. He gave a stiff nod, muttering, "Well, thanks." Then he turned and walked away, disappearing into one of the rooms.

While leaving Mr. Saroha's apartment Vishesh quickly sent the picture he had taken to a number saved in his phone as swargdoot.

Five minutes later, as Vishesh made his way down the hall, his phone buzzed. The voice on the other end was low and confirmed with certainty, "Yes, that's him. Confirmed."

A slow, satisfied smile spread across Vishesh's face. This was just the beginning.

Chapter 5

A Flight of Affection

It was a Sunday morning, nearly a week since Vishesh had read Maya's diary. Yet, in the back of his mind, he was still trying to figure out the right message to send her, something to initiate a conversation. There was an undeniable pull toward her that he couldn't ignore. As he pondered, he drove into the parking lot of the grocery store—and there she was. Maya.

His heart skipped a beat, and he couldn't help but giggle like a schoolboy. He quickly parked and rushed toward her, greeting her with excitement, "Hi, Maya!"

Maya turned, her face lighting up. "Oh, hi, Dr. Vishesh," she smiled warmly.

Vishesh, with a teasing grin, replied, "Did I call you 'software engineer Maya'?"

Maya chuckled. "Sorry, hi Vishesh, how are you?"

"All good," he said, and they began walking together.

From a distance, Smriti had been watching them. As Maya approached her, Smriti shot her a playful, knowing smile. "Hmm, something's going on here."

Maya's eyes widened, but she gave Smriti a shy smile and mouthed, "Shut up."

While they were at the checkout counter, Vishesh stood in the same line. Smriti, in the midst of the transaction, got a call from her boyfriend. He had just landed in Canada but she had forgotten to pick him up. Flustered, she turned to Maya. "Can I borrow your car? I need to get to the airport."

Before Maya could respond, Smriti turned to Vishesh. "Hey, Dr. Vishesh, could you drop Maya home? I'm taking her car. Thanks."

Vishesh stood silent for a moment, slightly puzzled. "Uh… sure," he finally said.

Maya, sensing the situation, hesitated. "No, it's fine, I'll just take a cab."

Vishesh quickly replied, "It's really no trouble, Maya. If you don't mind, I can drop you."

Maya didn't argue. She simply smiled in agreement.

As they drove, Maya noticed the quote again on the back mirror: "A soulmate doesn't necessarily mean a partner." Unable to resist, she asked, "What's the meaning of this quote?"

Vishesh smiled gently, glancing at her. "It's pretty self-explanatory, Maya. A soulmate doesn't always have to be your partner."

Maya raised an eyebrow. "Care to elaborate?"

Vishesh chuckled. "Alright, imagine a convex mirror. It's incomplete on its own, right? But when paired with another convex mirror, it becomes whole like a flame. A soulmate is like that: they complete you, but they're not always meant to be your partners."

Maya, still unsure, asked, "But how do I know when I've met my soulmate?"

Vishesh's tone softened. "There's no trick or technique. The right person will simply find you. And when they do, you'll feel something different, something you can't ignore."

Maya thought for a moment. "Hmm, if I can feel the difference, then why wouldn't I make that soulmate my partner?"

Vishesh smiled knowingly. "If you can, then you're lucky. But the truth is, soulmates are often meant to remain apart. Most of the time, they're not meant to be with you in the way a partner would."

Maya, unconvinced, turned her gaze out the window. "I don't agree. When there's no such thing as love, then soulmates are a myth," she said with a small laugh.

Vishesh looked at her with a mix of affection and kindness. After a pause, Maya noticed his gaze and nervously asked, "What? Is something wrong?"

Vishesh exhaled deeply. "Maya, I'm sorry, but I found your diary in my car…" he began.

Maya's face flushed with anger. "Did you read it?" she snapped.

Vishesh hesitated before replying, "Yes. Some pages."

Maya's expression hardened. "Please give it back. And stop the car. I'll manage from here."

Vishesh's voice was gentle but firm. "Maya, we're on the highway. I can't stop now. I know I crossed a line, but I only read a few pages—just three or four."

Maya fell silent.

Vishesh continued, his tone soft but earnest. "I don't know what happened with your last relationship, but trust me when I say this: love is the most beautiful thing in the world. Don't shut yourself off from it."

Maya remained quiet, her eyes downcast. Vishesh went on, his words carrying a deeper understanding. "Losing a boyfriend is painful, but I know it's not the breakup that's bothering you. It's your mother, isn't it?"

Maya closed her eyes, a wave of grief washing over her. Vishesh pulled the car into a parking spot they reached Maya's society, then turned to her. "I know I'm being too personal, but I can see the pain. Your mother… she left without you getting the chance to say goodbye. Maybe you had an argument with her before she passed. But you have to let go of that guilt. No matter what you said or didn't say, it wasn't your fault. Let it go, and life will be easier."

Maya's eyes shimmered with unshed tears as she glanced at him. She opened her mouth, but no words came. Finally, she whispered, "Things are always easier said than done. Anyway, thanks for the ride. Take care."

Vishesh watched her leave, his heart heavy. As she walked away, he muttered to himself, "Talk to me, Maya. I just want to help you let go of the burden."

After dinner, Smriti and Maya stood together on the balcony. Smriti was animated, recounting her meeting with her boyfriend, while Maya remained quiet, her thoughts lingering on what Vishesh had said earlier.

Suddenly, Maya broke the silence. "Sim, do you believe in love?"

Smriti, still caught up in the excitement of her story, replied, confused, "Of course, I do! I'm just telling you about my meetup with my boyfriend, whom I love."

Maya turned to her, the weight of her thoughts pressing down. "But do you consider him your soulmate?"

Smriti sighed, a small smile playing on her lips. "I guess so."

Maya's curiosity deepened. "How do you know he's your soulmate?"

Smriti shot her a playful look. "Did you watch some romantic movie or something?"

Maya softly smiled, "Tell me, Sim. How do you know?"

Smriti paused, her expression softening. "I don't know… he's just someone with whom I feel complete."

Maya's eyes narrowed as she pressed on, "You mean like you're two convex mirrors that complete a flame?"

Smriti laughed softly. "I'm not sure about mirrors, but yes… I just know that I can't hate him, even if I wanted to. He's like my second half—my soulmate."

Maya studied her friend, her expression calm yet questioning. "So, you'll do anything to marry him, right?"

Smriti averted her gaze and, as she turned to head inside, she muttered, "No."

Maya, confused, called after her, "But why? You just said he completes you, and now you're saying you won't marry him?"

Smriti's voice faltered. "It's not that I don't want to marry him. I do, Mimi, I really do. But his family won't accept me. He's made it clear… he's back from India, and you know what? He's engaged now."

The words hit Maya like a wave. Smriti's face crumpled, and tears began to fall. Maya rushed to her side, wrapping her in a tight hug. "I'm so sorry, Sim."

Through her tears, Smriti whispered, "Mimi… if you ever find your soulmate, just make them your partner. No matter what else happens, because if you don't, it's a lifetime of pain. Even if you marry someone else, you'll never stop thinking about your soulmate."

Maya stood silently, her heart heavy. As Smriti wiped her tears and moved toward the door, Maya lingered in thought, speaking softly to herself, "Do I even have a soulmate?"

Chapter 6

Unmasking the Mole

The next morning, Maya was working from home, as usual. Her roommate Smriti had already left for work, and Maya had back-to-back meetings on her calendar. It was just after 12:15 PM when the doorbell rang, pulling her attention away from her laptop. Still, on a Teams call, she moved toward the door, laptop in hand, her voice barely audible as she greeted the person on the other side.

It was Vishesh.

For a moment, she froze, staring at him as the voice from her call echoed, "Hello, Maya?" She quickly snapped back into the conversation. "Yes, I'm here," she said, mouthing to Vishesh to step inside.

Maya turned back to the call. "Tanay, can we continue this meeting in about 30 minutes? Also, can you send me the pictures from the team lunch?" She disconnected the call and turned to Vishesh. "Sorry about that. Please, make yourself comfortable."

Vishesh, looking slightly awkward, hesitated before replying, "It's fine, Maya. I just came to hand over your diary."

"Oh," Maya said, still a little distracted as she handed him a glass of water. "Thanks."

Vishesh took the water, his gaze lingering on her for a moment. "Okay, I'll take your leave now. I'm really sorry if any of my actions hurt you."

Maya looked at him quietly for a moment, then responded, "It's okay, Vishesh. We can get over this one."

He sighed in relief. "Uff, thanks."

She smiled softly. "Would you like some tea or coffee?"

Vishesh grinned, teasing, "Yes, hazelnut with almond milk, please."

Maya raised an eyebrow with a playful look. "Sorry, I don't have that one."

Vishesh laughed, the tension between them easing, and Maya smiled back, catching the glimmer of something in his eyes.

As Maya moved into the kitchen to make coffee, her laptop was sitting on the kitchen counter in front of Vishesh, still open with her Teams window active. Just then, a series of pictures from Tanay popped up. Vishesh glanced at them absentmindedly, but one photo caught his attention. It was of Maya with a girl and a guy. But it wasn't the girl that caught Vishesh's eye. It was the guy— the same man from Mr. Saroha's apartment.

Vishesh's eyes widened as he studied the photo, the recognition flashing in his mind. His expression remained carefully neutral, but his curiosity was piqued.

"Maya," he said, his voice steady but with a trace of tension, "You have some notifications on your Teams."

Maya placed a tray with two coffee mugs on the counter, smiling as she walked toward the laptop. "Oh, these are pictures from the day you saw me at the gas station," she said with a laugh. "Remember?"

Vishesh looked at the name in the Teams window: Tanay Awasthi. He couldn't resist asking, trying to keep his tone casual, "Who's that girl with you? She looks cute. What's her name?"

Maya shot him a sidelong glance, raising an eyebrow. Vishesh, noticing her look, quickly added, "Just asking, generally."

Maya smirked. "There's a guy too. You didn't think to ask his name?"

Vishesh laughed awkwardly, then shrugged. "Okay, fine. Tell me the names of both."

Maya paused for a moment before answering. "She's Avantika, and he's Tanay. They both work in my team."

Vishesh mulled over the names, his mind already working, but he kept his thoughts to himself. After a few more minutes of casual conversation, he finished his coffee and stood up to leave. "I'll let you get back to work," he said, offering a polite smile.

Maya nodded, and they exchanged a few more pleasantries before he walked out.

As soon as he reached his car, Vishesh pulled out his phone and dialed a number.

"Stay vigilant the path is clearing," he ordered, his voice calm but with a hint of urgency.

After hanging up, he sent a quick message: "Tanay Awasthi."

Later that evening, after finishing her dinner, Maya stood on her balcony, enjoying the cool night air when her phone chimed. She picked it up and saw a message from Vishesh: "Oh no, last time I said the next coffee would be on me, but today again it was from you. Can I get another chance to pay for your coffee?"

Maya smiled to herself, her cheeks flushing slightly as she typed a reply: "Maya - 2, Vishesh - 0. The result says it all, so the winner deserves more than just coffee."

Barely two minutes later, another message popped up, accompanied by a wink emoji: "True, the winner deserves a dinner instead."

Maya laughed softly, shaking her head and typing. "Chill, Vishesh. I was just kidding."

Vishesh responded instantly, his tone playful: "Well, I'm not. Tell me a place."

Maya hesitated, the surprise clear on her face, but there was also a trace of shyness. Finally, she typed: "I'll let you know after checking my schedule."

Vishesh replied with a smile emoji: "Sure, I'll be waiting."

The silence in Vishesh's apartment was broken by the sharp buzz of a phone call. He glanced at the screen and answered, his expression unreadable. The voice on the other side was low, almost ominous:

"We got her. You can start working on your plan now."

Vishesh's fingers tightened around the phone as his mind raced. He said nothing, his thoughts swirling, as the weight of the words settled deep within him. This was just the beginning.

Chapter 7

A Web of Secrets

---

*T*he car came to a halt in front of an isolated, abandoned building, two men dressed in Indian Army uniforms stepped out, their faces set with purpose. Moments later, a woman, also in uniform, emerged, firmly holding a girl whose hands were tied, mouth taped, and eyes blindfolded. They entered a dimly lit room. The lady officer named, Shreya Bhattacharya, guided the girl to the chair, securing her legs to its frame before untying her hands and peeling the tape from her mouth. Finally, she removed the blindfold, revealing a pair of piercing, angry eyes glaring at her.

Shreya met the defiant gaze with calm authority, offering a glass of water. "What's your name?" she asked. The girl turned her head away in silent defiance refusing the offer. Shreya's patience faltered, and with a swift slap, she forced the girl to face her. "Tell me your name and what you were doing at the cyber cafe," she demanded.

The girl's voice, steady and unapologetic, cut through the tension. "My name is Shahista and since when has it become a crime to visit a cyber cafe?"

"Daily?" Shreya pressed; her tone sharp. Shahista's silence was loud enough to speak for her.

Shreya leaned forward, her eyes narrowing. "You must have a smartphone. After the repeal of Article 370, internet access is hardly an issue anymore. So why the cyber cafe?"

A bitter smile tugged at Shahista's lips. "Article 370's repeal? Who asked for it?" she replied, her tone unapologetic and fierce.

Shreya saw an opening and thought of using Shahista's anger. "So, you're saying you preferred the curfews, the violence, the fear in the valley?"

Shahista's anger erupted like a storm. "This is our valley! Don't try to lecture us what we need!" she shouted.

Shreya's palm slammed against the table, the sound reverberating through the room. "Answer my question," she said, her voice sharp and commanding. "Why the cyber cafe?"

Shahista's fiery look, dimmed momentarily, "Because my father wants to separate me from my boyfriend," she said quietly, her tone bitter. "He took my phone away."

Shreya quickly pulled out her phone and slid it across the table toward Shahista. The screen displays an image of Tanay Awasthi. "Is he your boyfriend?" she demanded, her tone calm but laced with authority. Shahista, still stubborn and refusing to cooperate, turned her head away.

Frustrated, Shreya leaned forward, gripping Shahista's face firmly. "Answer my questions," she said, her voice cold and deliberate, "or in the next thirty minutes, your father will be sitting in the chair right next to yours."

At this, Shahista's composure cracked. Her face turned pale, and fear flickered in her eyes. "Not my father," she pleaded, her voice trembling. "He's innocent. He knows nothing."

Shreya leaned towards Shashita, her finger now pointing directly at the image on her phone. "Then start talking. Is he your boyfriend?" she asked again. This time, Shahista hesitated before nodding her head in agreement.

Without missing a beat, Shreya fired her next question. "What's his name, and how do you know him?"

Shahista let out a shaky breath, "His name is Salman," she began. "We studied at the same college. He was brilliant, always top of the class, but he wasn't financially stable. To support himself, he gave tuition. I was one of his students… and that's how it started. That's when we fell in love."

Canada

Maya decided to visit the office today, feeling bored at home. However, when she arrived, only Tanay and Mr. Thomas from marketing were present. She greeted them warmly, saying, "Hi guys, I was getting bored, so I thought I should visit the office today. But it seems I chose the wrong day." Mr. Thomas chuckled and replied, "Post-COVID, it's just me and Tanay who come to the office daily. The rest show up whenever they feel like it." Maya smiled and settled into her seat. Mr. Thomas occupied a cubicle nearby, while Tanay worked at a desk near the conference room.

Around 3:30 PM, Mr. Thomas left for the day. Later, at around 4:30 PM, Maya stood up to pack her things. "Okay, Tanay, I'll take my leave. I want to reach home before it gets dark," she said. Tanay smiled and responded, "Alright, Maya. See you around. I'll stay a little longer for a presentation. It's hard to focus at home since I live with my landlords."

Maya left the office but decided to grab a coffee before heading home. While paying, she realized she had left her wallet on her desk. She returned to retrieve it and, as she was leaving, noticed Tanay in the conference room.

The TV screen displayed several random chat windows, visible because the blinds were partially open. She glanced at Tanay's desk and saw his office laptop there, which puzzled her. "Which system is he using?" she wondered. Suddenly, she heard Tanay speaking on the phone, "I have sent three new pieces today. This will complete the message to execute the plan." Intrigued, Maya focused on the screen and saw three maps displayed. Just then, Tanay's gaze met hers. Panic surged through her as she bolted from the office. Luckily, her car was parked near the gate. She jumped in, started the engine, and drove away as fast as she could, unsure if Tanay was following her.

Terrified and unsure who to trust, Maya called Vishesh. "Vishesh," she said breathlessly. Hearing her shaky voice, Vishesh immediately asked, "Maya, are you okay? What happened?" Struggling to speak, she said, "Someone is following me." Vishesh's tone turned serious. "Who is following you? What's going on?" Maya hesitated before responding, "I might have discovered something dangerous." Before she could continue, Vishesh interrupted, "Is it about Tanay?" Shocked, Maya asked, "How do you know?"

Avoiding her question, Vishesh said firmly, "Maya, listen to me carefully. Do not go home. I'm sending you, my address. Tell me how far you are." She checked her location and replied, "About 25 minutes away." Vishesh instructed her, "Download the map offline and turn off your phone and when you are here, take the back gate of the building. I'll be waiting there, but don't turn your phone on unless I tell you to do so."

Exactly 25 minutes later, Maya arrived at the back gate, where Vishesh was anxiously waiting. As soon as she stepped out of the car, three men approached and got into her vehicle. Confused, she looked at Vishesh, who reassured her, "Don't worry, Maya. These are my men." Overwhelmed with fear and relief, Maya ran to Vishesh and hugged him tightly. He held her close, rubbing her back to calm her. "I've got you, Maya. I won't let anything happen to you," he whispered.

Maya glanced back and saw the man driving her car was the same junkies she had seen at the gas station earlier. She decided not to mention it, trusting Vishesh completely. Without further hesitation, she followed him through the fire exit and into the safety of the building.

Chapter 8

The Other Vishesh

Through the fire exit, Maya and Vishesh climbed the staircase and entered his apartment. As they stepped inside, Maya froze in shock. Sitting on the sofa was a man who looked exactly like Vishesh. She turned toward him, her face a mixture of confusion and disbelief. "What is going on?" she demanded, her voice trembling. Vishesh reached out to hold her, trying to calm her. "Maya, let me explain," he said gently. But she resisted, stepping back. "No! What is this? Who is he?" she asked, her fear palpable.

The man on the sofa stood up, his demeanor calm yet commanding. "Maya," he said, "I'm Dr. Vishesh Khurana, and this," he pointed to Vishesh standing beside her, "is my identical twin brother, Major Arjun Khurana."

Maya's eyes darted between the two men, trying to process what she was hearing. She turned to Arjun, bewildered. He stepped forward, his tone firm but sincere. "Yes, Maya, I'm Arjun. Let me explain everything from the beginning. "I landed in Canada on the same day you had your dental appointment. You met Vishesh at the reception, but I was the one waiting in the cabin. That's why Dona was hesitant to let you in—she was trying to give hints to Vishesh to refuse your appointment. But you came in anyway. I hid in the closet while Vishesh treated you. After your appointment, while your eyes were closed, I sent Vishesh to leave for Vancouver and stayed behind. I was the one who handed you the receipt."

Maya's voice shook as she asked, "Then who was it at the gas station? At the coffee shop? The grocery store? And who came to my house?"

Arjun locked eyes with her, his gaze filled with emotions. "It was me, Maya. Initially, at the clinic, you were just another patient. But that night at the gas station, I was there with my men, waiting for someone as we got a lead, but you arrived unexpectedly, so I had to change my plan quickly. But fate had other plans. The incident with the car became my reason to see you again."

Before he could continue, Maya interrupted, her voice rising. "What about the grocery store? And my house? Was it you or Vishesh there?"

Vishesh interrupted, "I just met you only once, at the clinic's reception where you gave me that cool vibe, "he smiled while saying just trying to lighten the mood.

Arjun took a step closer and gently placed his hands on her shoulders, his tone earnest. "Maya, I'm not a man who sugarcoats words. I need to be straightforward with you—I've developed feelings for you. It started when I read your diary. I saw your vulnerability, and your strength when you gave that old man a befitting reply, and I couldn't help but feel drawn to you. At your house, it was me. I wanted to come clean about who I am and what I feel for you. But then, I saw Tanay's picture."

Maya's eyes widened in fear. "Tanay?" she whispered; her voice barely audible. Panic began to creep into her expression. "Who is he? What could he do? He knows where I live! Oh no—Smriti is alone at home! What if he tries to harm her?"

Arjun quickly grabbed his phone and dialed a number, "Stay near Maya's apartment and keep an eye on everything," he instructed. As soon as the call ended, he turned to Vishesh "You go too, stay there and keep me posted ", Vishesh left in a hurry.

Tanay stepped out of an Uber, standing just outside Maya's building. Walking towards the parking lot to access the elevator, he was unaware that the three men who had driven Maya's car earlier were watching him from a distance. One of them phoned Arjun. "He's here," the man reported. "Approaching Maya's apartment."

Arjun immediately called Vishesh. "It's time. Get into Maya's apartment and stay with Smriti. But don't tell her anything."

Vishesh reached the building just as Tanay entered the elevator. The two locked eyes and Tanay's expression shifted to surprise. Vishesh smiled casually. "Oh, hi! Remember me? I came to deliver groceries to your place. I'm your neighbor."

Tanay gave a blank smile, hiding his confusion. "Oh, yes... of course."

The elevator ride was tense, and when they both stepped out on the same floor, Tanay stopped to watch Vishesh head toward Maya's apartment. "Are you going to flat 306?" Tanay asked, trying to sound casual. Vishesh turned slightly and nodded. "Yes, my girlfriend lives here."

Tanay froze, visibly shocked. "You mean Maya Sharma is your girlfriend?" he asked, trying to mask his disbelief.

Vishesh grinned. "Yes. Why? Is there a problem?"

Tanay quickly composed himself. "No, nothing at all. I was just going to see her too. I'm taking a long leave, so I thought I'd hand over some of my pending tasks."

Vishesh nodded and rang the bell. "Oh, okay."

Smriti opened the door, looking anxious. "Dr. Vishesh! And Tanay?" she said, her voice trembling.

Vishesh frowned. "What happened, Smriti?"

She looked worried. "Maya isn't back yet, and it's already 10 PM. Her phone is switched off too."

Tanay's brow furrowed. "What do you mean? She left the office at 4:30. Where else could she go except home?"

Vishesh kept his composure. "I spoke to her earlier. She told me to meet her here. Let me call and check."

Dialing Arjun, Vishesh said aloud, "Hi, Maya. When will you be back? Tanay is here too. He wants to give you a handover."

On the other end, Arjun quickly instructed, "tell them she's gone to Mississauga for 3 days to visit her cousin, who is sick. Then stay in the building."

Following Arjun's directions, Vishesh calmly said, "Oh, Maya told me she went to Mississauga to see her cousin. She'll be back in 2-3 days."

Hearing this, Tanay had no choice but to leave, though suspicion lingered in his eyes. After he walked away, Vishesh stepped out, positioning himself discreetly near the apartment, just as Arjun had advised.

Back in the safe house, Arjun handed Maya a glass of water. She looked at him uneasily. "Tanay is at home.

Why are you asking Vishesh to leave knowing Tanay is standing there at my building?"

Arjun met her gaze with a steady calmness. "Maya, trust me. With Vishesh seeing Tanay at your apartment, he won't dare make any moves tonight. Vishesh is there, my team is nearby, and nothing will happen. Tanay will search everywhere to find you, but not his own building. This is the safest place for you right now."

Maya lay in Arjun's room, staring at the ceiling, unable to sleep. The weight of the day's events pressed heavily on her mind. After tossing and turning for hours, she finally got up and stepped into the hall to get some water. Her movements alerted Arjun, who had been lightly dozing on the couch. He immediately sat up. "What happened, Maya? Are you okay?" he asked, concern etched across his face.

"I can't sleep," she admitted, her voice barely above a whisper.

Arjun stood and gestured toward the sofa near the window. "Come sit with me. You can talk to me, Maya. Do you want to tell me, what you saw today?"

Maya hesitated but then nodded. "I saw Tanay sending something to someone."

"What was he sending, and to whom?" Arjun leaned forward; his tone serious.

"I'm not 100% sure," Maya said, furrowing her brows as she tried to piece the memory together. "I think they were images of maps. He sent them to three different people in three different chat windows."

Arjun's expression hardened. "Do you remember anything else? Was there anything written on the maps? Or do you recall the names on the chat windows?"

Maya closed her eyes, concentrating. "I think… I think one of the names was Fatima, and the other was Zooni. I couldn't catch the third name. By that time, he saw me, and I ran away." She shivered slightly, her voice quivering as the memory resurfaced.

Arjun noticed her distress, and without hesitation, he moved closer and gently wrapped his arms around her. "You did a great job, Maya. You might not realize it, but what you saw today could save lives."

Maya pulled back slightly, her eyes wide with a mixture of fear and confusion. "Who is Tanay, Arjun? What is he up to? And why are you here?"

Chapter 9

The Pigeon's Warning

*J*ust three months before Arjun's arrival to Canada. At that time, Arjun was posted in the Kashmir Valley, one afternoon, as he sat enjoying lunch with his friends, a familiar figure appeared—a local shepherd who doubled as an informant for the army. This man, known for his knack for uncovering hidden secrets, was affectionately nicknamed "Kabootar" (Pigeon) by Arjun. Kabootar approached with urgency in his steps. Spotting him, Arjun immediately put down his plate and asked, "What happened?" Kabootar leaned in, his voice low but firm, and said, "Something is in the works. Check with Aftab Coaching Classes." Without waiting for a response, he turned and left, leaving Arjun to process the cryptic warning.

Later that day, around 4 PM, Arjun decided to investigate. Dressed in civilian clothes, he headed to a tea stall near Aftab Coaching Classes, blending into the bustling surroundings. From his vantage point, he noticed that most of the students entering the coaching center were girls of a similar age group. Curious, he struck up a casual conversation with the tea stall owner. "Is this coaching center only for girls?" he asked. The stall owner shook his head. "No, sir, it's just a rented space. Different tutors use it. Between 4 and 6 PM, though, it's a girls-only batch."

The next day, acting on Arjun's instructions, Captain Shreya visited the coaching center, also dressed in civilian attire. As she walked up to the reception desk, she smiled and said, "Hi, I'd like to know the fees. I'm considering enrolling my younger sister." The receptionist, a middle-aged woman with a polite demeanor, asked, "Girls-only batch or co-ed?" "Girls-only," Shreya responded casually. While the receptionist looked up details in the system, Shreya seized the opportunity to explore. "Can you point me to the washroom?" she asked, hoping to observe the premises.

As she wandered through the corridors, Shreya's attention was drawn to a corner where a guy stood talking to a girl. Something about the interaction felt off. She watched as the boy handed the girl a small paper slip. The girl quickly tucked it away, her behavior jittery. Moments later, the boy slipped out of the building, and the girl followed soon after, almost in a rush. Sensing something amiss, Shreya decided to trail the girl, though she couldn't catch a clear glimpse of the boy, but the girl was none other than Shahista.

Shreya followed Shahista from a safe distance, Shahista eventually entered a small cybercafé, and Shreya discreetly noted the location before reporting her findings to Arjun. The next day, Arjun and Shreya positioned themselves near Aftab Coaching Classes, observing the premises from afar during the 4–6 PM slot. Their observations revealed a pattern—Shahista consistently left the class 15 minutes early and headed straight to the cybercafé.

Nearly a week later, while Arjun was in the market, Kabootar approached him again, his tone somber. "So many innocent girls are being used in the name of love," he said. "Hawaon mein bagawat hai." With those cryptic words, Kabootar disappeared once more, leaving Arjun to piece together the implications.

Shreya intensified her surveillance, determined to uncover the truth. One day, she spotted the mysterious boy again, this time handing a slip to another girl. Though she attempted to follow him, he vanished into the crowd midway. The team later discovered that the tea stall owner had been tipping off the mysterious boy, warning him whenever someone was observing or following him. Despite this setback, Shreya managed to catch the new girl the boy had approached.

The slip the girl received was retrieved and revealed a cryptic message: "Cash and Numbers and Different Amount N##3{{R]]7@@A**2, 5 Not 5 Golden Gates" When questioned, the girl explained that the tutor—the mysterious boy—had instructed her to send the message to a specific Facebook account. He had also mentioned that he would be leaving town for a few days.

The team worked tirelessly to decode the meaning of the slip. After hours of effort, the team finally cracked it: taking the first letters of each word—C, A, N, A, D, and A—spelled out "CANADA." The message implied that the cash, currency, and amount would soon be different, hinting that the tutor was planning to leave for Canada soon and that his address would be Flat no 505 Golden Gates Society, N3R 7A2, Burlington Canada.

Present Day Vishesh's Apartment

Maya sat silently by the window, lost in her thoughts. Arjun entered the room with a tray of breakfast and gently placed it beside her. "Maya," he said softly, sitting down next to her, "I know this is a difficult phase for you, but you're safe now."

Maya turned to him; her eyes filled with doubt. "How do I know I should believe you?" she asked. "Since last night, I can't make sense of anything. What did you mean when you said I might have saved lives?"

Arjun sighed deeply. "Maya," he began, "Tanay is a criminal. He's using innocent girls to deliver messages to his terror groups. He manipulates his classmates and students, makes them fall in love with him, and hides behind them to avoid suspicion. He's planning something big, and I'm close to finding out what it is. Trust me, I'll tell you everything when the time is right, but you have to believe me. Everything I'm doing, I've thought through carefully."

Maya stood up slowly, her expression softening. She hugged Arjun, this time consciously and firmly. "I trust you, Arjun," she said. "I'll stay strong so you can focus on catching him without worrying about me."

Arjun smiled and hugged her back. "Don't worry about me, I can multitask. Just finish your breakfast. Around noon, Dona will be here with new clothes for you. Let me know if you need anything else."

Present Day Kashmir

Shreya leaned forward; her gaze fixed on Shahista. "What exactly did Salman ask you to do?" she asked firmly. Shahista, who had initially been resistant, now appeared defeated, her voice barely above a whisper. "He gives me messages to deliver further," she admitted.

"What kind of messages?" Shreya pressed.

"Sometimes written messages," Shahista hesitated before continuing, "sometimes images… of maps."

Before Shreya could probe further, her phone buzzed, breaking the tense silence. It was Arjun on the line. His voice was urgent. "Three new names, two confirmed, find Zooni and Fatima. They have three more pieces—a major clue to the plan. We're running out of time."

Shreya without wasting any minute called his teammates and passed on the message she got from Arjun and then turned back to Shahista, gripping her face gently but firmly. "What's the plan?" she demanded. Shahista winced, resisting the pain. "I don't know," she replied weakly. "I just know there are more pieces of maps I have to send, but… you caught me."

Shreya narrowed her eyes. "Who are you sending these messages to?"

"There's no name," Shahista muttered. "Every time it's a different ID."

"What kind of IDs?" Shreya pressed.

"It's like User57, User89… no names, no faces," Shahista explained.

Shreya shifted her tone, her voice edged with sarcasm. "Who else is working for Salman? Any other girls?"

"No!" Shahista protested, shaking her head. "Salman loves me. He said he'll marry me."

Shreya let out a mocking laugh. "Oh? And when's the wedding? Where is your Salman now?"

"He's abroad," Shahista responded defensively. "He'll come back soon… once he has enough money to execute his plans and goals."

Shreya leaned in closer, her voice dropping. "What goals?"

Before Shahista could answer, two officers entered the room with Zooni and Fatima, both blindfolded and tied. Shreya quickly helped them into chairs and secured their legs before removing the blindfolds. As the cloth slipped away, Shreya was startled to see that Zooni was just 14 years old. The girl was trembling with fear.

Shreya knelt beside her, offering a glass of water and patting her head gently. "Don't be afraid," she said softly. "I just need to ask a few questions, and then you can go. Do you know Salman?"

Zooni's eyes darted to Shahista before she gave a hesitant nod.

Noticing the subtle glance, Shreya asked, "Do you know these girls?"

"Yes," Zooni replied nervously. "My mom works as a receptionist at their coaching class."

Shreya's tone remained calm but probing. "Did Salman send you any images yesterday?"

Zooni hesitated, her lips trembling. Shreya placed a comforting hand on her shoulder. "It's okay. Don't be scared. I'm here to help."

Finally, Zooni spoke. "Yes, maps. He asked me to give the printouts to my mom."

Shahista's eyes widened in shock, glaring at Zooni. Shreya immediately turned to her, her voice fierce. "You tell me what Salman's plan is, or I swear I'll make you regret it."

Before Shahista could respond, Fatima burst into tears. "Salman is a monster!" she cried. "He said he loved me. He kept chatting with me, but last night he sent me a map and told me to prove my love to him I have to pass the printouts to Shahista. I went to the coaching class to find Shahista, I overheard some men talking to the receptionist."

Shreya leaned in; her curiosity piqued. "What were they saying?"

"They were asking if the receptionist's daughter had handed over the map yet," Fatima explained. "They said they needed it to start preparing for the execution. One of them said, 'Salman Bhai will give the command any day now. We can't fail. This is our valley, and we have to show the Indian government that Kashmir isn't theirs to rule as they please.'"

Shreya handed Fatima a glass of water and asked gently, "What did you do after that?"

"Nothing," Fatima replied, her voice shaking. "I left. I don't want to be part of any violence. Things are getting better here, and I want that to continue."

Shreya turned to both girls. "Do you have the printouts?"

They nodded, and with their cooperation, the team retrieved the missing pieces of the map. Soon after, another map was uncovered through Shahista's Facebook messages. The puzzle was finally coming together.

Vishesh's Apartment

Arjun's phone buzzed, displaying the name Swargdoot. He answered swiftly. "Yes, what's the update?"

Shreya's voice came through the line. "We've got all the pieces, but according to Fatima, Salman's orders are still pending, and what about the third girl? What's our next move?

There was a pause on the other end before Arjun spoke. "Nothing for now. Stay alert and keep monitoring the areas indicated on the maps. I'll handle Tanay— aka Salman."

Shreya frowned. "How?"

Arjun didn't answer immediately. Instead, he turned toward Maya, who sat nearby. His gaze lingered on her as if a plan slowly taking shape in his mind.

Chapter 10

The Plan

Arjun's eyes lingered on Maya as he spoke over the phone with Shreya. Sensing his unease, Maya approached him, her voice soft yet firm. "What happened, Arjun? Is everything okay?"

Arjun ended the call after saying, "Get Zooni's mother. She will lead us to something. I'll trap Salman." Turning his full attention to Maya, he gently held her hand and guided her to the couch. With a concerned expression, he began, "Maya, I need your help. But before anything, I need you to understand the risk involved."

He took a deep breath before continuing. "Tanay isn't who you think he is. His real name is Salman, a Kashmiri militant. He's been using innocent girls to pass messages to his terror groups. Thanks to you, we tracked down Zooni and Fatima and identified areas where they were planning to execute their next move. But, Maya, we still don't know what that plan is. And there's only one person who can tell us."

Maya cut in, her tone steady and determined, "And that's Salman himself."

"Correct," Arjun replied, meeting her gaze. "Maya, I know this is dangerous. I wouldn't ask you if there were another way. But we need to trap Salman, and for that, I need your help."

Without hesitation, Maya nodded, her resolve unwavering. "I'll do it, Arjun. I'll help you stop Salman and bring his plans to light."

Relief washed over Arjun as he pulled her into an embrace. "Thank you, Maya. I promise you, no matter what, I won't let anything happen to you."

Kashmir

Shreya was still seated with Shashita, Fatima, and Zooni when her phone rang. It was her colleague. The news was grim—Zooni's mother was not at the coaching center or her house.

Taking a moment to process, Shreya moved closer to Zooni. "Zooni," she began gently, "is there any other place where your mother could be?"

Zooni remained silent, her gaze fixed on the floor. Shreya pulled up a chair and sat beside her, her voice calm but firm. "Do you want to save your mother?"

Zooni hesitated before nodding slightly.

"Then tell me what you know," Shreya said. "If you don't, the army might mistake her for a terrorist and she could be killed in an encounter."

Zooni's resolve broke. Tears streamed down her face as she whispered, "You can check the public library. I'm not sure, but whenever she senses trouble, she goes there."

Shreya leaned in, her curiosity piqued. "And how do you know she goes to the library?"

Zooni wiped her tears and explained, "Once, a parent came to the coaching center, furious. Their daughter wasn't coming home on time because she was seeing a boy from the coaching center. They accused my mom of running a scam and threatened to report her to the police. She got scared and went to the library. I know this because I followed her that day—I was scared she might find out about me talking to Salman."

"And what did she do at the library?" Shreya asked, her voice steady.

"She had a phone with her," Zooni replied, her voice breaking. "She used it to call someone."

"Who did she call?" Shreya pressed.

"I don't know anything else," Zooni sobbed. "Please, just save my mom,"

Shreya called her colleagues and asked them to check the library.

<hr>

Vishesh's Apartment

Arjun picked up his phone and called Vishesh. "Are you still in the building?" he asked.

"Yes, I'm in the laundry room," Vishesh replied.

"Good. Now leave the building through the front door while we're on this call. Run as if you're in a hurry and then come home," Arjun instructed. Vishesh, without hesitation, did as told.

Fifteen minutes later, Vishesh burst into the apartment. "Oh, that was a hell of a night, bro. Hi, Maya," he greeted, collapsing onto the couch.

Arjun didn't give him a moment to rest. "Don't get comfortable yet—you're going back. Maya, come here too, and bring your phone."

Arjun immediately called his team. "Bring Maya's car back to my building and park it in the parking lot," he ordered with urgency in his voice.

"So, what's the plan?" Vishesh asked, a hint of surprise in his tone.

Without wasting a moment, Arjun switched on Maya's phone and handed it to Vishesh. "Take this and drive

Maya's car. If Salman is tracking Maya, the moment he detects her phone signal, he'll assume she's in the car and will try to chase it. Your job is to distract him."

Then, turning to Maya, he asked, "Maya, I want you to go to Mr.Saroha's apartment and search Salman's room for anything laptop tablet or phone".

Maya hesitated for a second before replying," Okay"

Vishesh sprinted downstairs, wasting no time. Meanwhile, Arjun quickly called Dona, who was already waiting near the entrance. Without hesitation, Vishesh and Dona got into Maya's car and drove out through the building's front gate. The moment they exited, Salman, who had been keeping a watchful eye, spotted the car. Seeing a man and a woman inside, he immediately assumed it was Maya. His suspicion was further confirmed when he noticed Dona wearing a scarf that concealed her face. Without a second thought, Salman began tailing them.

Mr. Saroha's Apartment

As per Arjun's plan, Maya was tasked with searching Salman's room. She rang Mr. Saroha's doorbell, and the house answered. Maya gave a polite smile and said, "Hi, is Mrs. Saroha home? I'm Shashita, I am Tanay's friend".

The household called for Mrs. Saroha, who soon appeared. "Yes?" she asked.

Maya smiled warmly, hiding the nervousness bubbling inside. "Hi, Mrs. Saroha, I'm Shahista, Tanay's friend. Is he home?"

Mrs. Saroha hesitated for a moment before replying, "Let me call Tanay. He's not home right now." As she picked up the phone to dial, Maya's heart raced, but she kept her composure, masking her fear behind a calm smile. Thankfully, Tanay disconnected the call.

"I'm only here because my mom sent a parcel from India for me and Tanay picked it up on my behalf," Maya explained. "I came to collect it."

Mrs. Saroha thought for a moment, but before she could respond, the doorbell rang again. This time, it was the building's security guard, who seemed flustered.

"Mrs. Saroha, there's an urgent society meeting in the hall, and you've been called for it," he informed her.

"What happened?" she asked, concerned.

"The fire exit was found broken. It seems like some junkies may have broken the metal handle. The meeting is just to ensure everyone's safety," the guard explained.

(Arjun, after sending Vishesh and Maya on their decoy mission, had gone downstairs, broke the fire exit gate himself, and instructed the security guard—one of his own team members—to call for an emergency meeting.)

Mrs. Saroha, clearly worried, turned to the house help. "Just open Tanay's room and help the lady get what she's looking for," she instructed before hurrying off with the guard.

Maya stepped into Tanay's room, her heart pounding as she took in the modest space. The house help lingered by the door; her curious eyes fixed on Maya's every move. Desperately searching for any clue, Maya's gaze darted around the room, but there was no sign of any gadgets, then she crouched down and peered under the bed, her breath catching when she spotted a dusty box pushed into the shadows. Forcing herself to remain calm, she slid the box out and opened it. Inside was a diary and an old laptop. Sensing the house help's suspicion, Maya quickly straightened up and flashed a casual smile. "Oh, there it is," she said, holding up the laptop and diary. "I'm a student here, so these are for my studies." Her voice was light, but her mind was racing. She could feel the weight of the house help's gaze, and she knew she had to act normal—no matter what she had just uncovered. Without arousing suspicion, she walked out of the room and left the apartment, clutching the items tightly. Inside, her nerves were on edge.

Community hall

The residents of the building gathered in the hall, their voices filled with concern and curiosity. People whispered among themselves, wondering what had happened and if everyone was safe. Just then, Arjun entered, with a bandage wrapped around his left arm. He raised his hand to calm the crowd. "Please, everyone, settle down," he said confidently. "I'm Dr. Vishesh from apartment 503. It was a group of junkies. I saw them sneaking into the building with the intention of robbery. I confronted them, and during the scuffle, I got a little injured." He gestured to his arm. "But don't worry, they ran off, and there's no serious damage. I called this meeting to make sure everyone stays vigilant. Please ensure your doors are locked during the nights, as it will take a couple of days to fix the fire exit door."

Vishesh's Apartment

Arjun pushed open the door to find Maya pacing nervously. The moment she saw him, she ran to him and hugged him tightly. Arjun hugged her back, sensing her tension.

"What's wrong with your arm?" she asked, her voice trembling with shock.

"Nothing—it's fake," Arjun reassured her with a small smile. "Did you find anything?"

Maya quickly pulled out the laptop and the diary she had taken.

"Great job, Maya," Arjun said, nodding with approval. "Now, pack the essentials. We have 15 minutes to leave the building because Salman will be back soon."

Kashmir

Meanwhile, Shreya and her team had brought Zooni's mother, Atifa, from the library. Her phone had been confiscated, and Shreya wasted no time in interrogating her.

"What's Salman's plan?" Shreya demanded, her voice sharp and commanding.

Atifa, visibly shaken, tried to defend herself. "I don't know anything"!!

Frustrated, Shreya slapped her across the face, her patience wearing thin. "Tell me the plan right now, or I'll have your daughter executed as an accomplice!"

Atifa broke down, tears streaming down her face. "On the 17th of October, the government is inaugurating a CBSE-affiliated school in Kashmir," she admitted, trembling. "It's a school that isn't Urdu-specific. They're trying to bring Kashmir in line with the rest of India's education system. But we don't want that—we need to protect our ethics and principles. We won't let them open that school!"

"What are you planning to do?" Shreya pressed further; her tone relentless.

"We're planning bomb blasts to spread fear and stop people from supporting the school," Atifa confessed, her voice cracking. "Salman already sent us the target areas— the school, the big ground near the masjid, the main market and the subzi mandi. These are the most crowded spots. The bombs have already been planted, and we're just waiting for Salman's command."

Shreya narrowed her eyes. "And what's with the phone?"

Atifa hesitated before answering. "Salman will call on this phone and tell us the exact time to leave the places as the bombs will detonate on their own on the 17th of October."

Shreya turned to an officer standing by the gate. "What's the date today?" she asked sharply.

"It's the 15th of October," the officer replied.

Shreya's jaw tightened. They only had two days to stop the catastrophe.

Chapter 11

The Chain Reaction

October 16th Kashmir

Shreya and her team leaned over the scattered pieces of the map, their eyes scanning for any overlooked detail. Suddenly, Yuvraj, a young and observant officer, pointed to the arrangement with a spark of realization. "Look! All four areas where the bombs are planted are within a 2-kilometer radius. It's like… a pattern," he said, his voice cutting through the tense silence.

Shreya turned to him sharply, her brow furrowed. "What pattern?" she asked, her tone demanding clarity.

Yuvraj quickly explained, gesturing to the map. "Spot 1 is the school, which is about 500 meters from the ground near the masjid. From the masjid, the main market is another 750 meters, and from the market, the sabzi mandi is another 750 meters. Add it up, and the total radius is 2 kilometers."

Shreya's mind raced as she questioned, "But why would they plant four bombs within just a 2-kilometer radius? Something's missing. This doesn't add up."

Before anyone could respond, the room stiffened as Colonel Shekhar Ahlawat stepped in. The team instinctively stood at attention. "At ease, team," the commanding officer said in his authoritative yet calm voice. "What's the update? And can someone connect me to Arjun, please?"

(Col Ahlawat was the commanding officer and Arjun was a part of his team, When the team decoded the slip that stated Canada and through the sources and the girl Shreya had captured confirmed that Salman had moved to Canada, Ahlawat sent Arjun to catch Salman in Canada).

Hotel Niagara Inn, Canada

Arjun sat at the edge of the bed, flipping through Salman's diary while Maya worked furiously to unlock the laptop they had recovered. The tension was palpable.

"It's asking for a password, Arjun," Maya said, glancing at him anxiously.

Arjun rubbed his chin, thinking aloud. "What could the password be? It has to be related to the mission…"

Maya hesitated, then suggested, "Maybe… the name of their mission?"

Before Arjun could respond, his phone buzzed. It was a video call from Shreya. Answering, he saw her face, tense but focused. "Hi, Arjun Sir. Colonel Shekhar Ahlawat is here," she said, stepping aside to reveal the Colonel standing behind her.

"Hello, Arjun," Colonel Ahlawat greeted, his voice steady. "Any progress in Canada?"

Arjun straightened in his chair; his tone professional. "Yes, Sir. We've identified the possible locations and the motive. The plan involves multiple blasts in order to object the opening of a CBSE school by creating tension and terror amongst the people. "

Ahlawat turned to the team. "Have we located the bombs yet?"

Yuvraj stepped forward. "Not yet, Sir, but we're actively on it." "Be quick the clock is ticking now we are just a day away from 17th October.!

Arjun added, "Sir, we recovered a laptop and a diary from Salman's apartment. Maya is working on unlocking it now." He turned the camera toward Maya. "This is Maya."

Ahlawat's stern demeanor softened as he nodded. "Thank you, Maya, for your courage and help. Thanks to your efforts, we've been able to track down critical leads."

Maya gave a small smile, brushing off the praise. "There's no need to thank me, It's my responsibility."

Arjun interjected; his voice sharp with urgency. "Shreya, go back to the women you questioned earlier. Ask them if they know what this mission is called. It might be the key to the password."

Shreya nodded. "Yes, Sir."

As the call ended, the room fell into a heavy silence. The clock was ticking, and every second mattered. Maya glanced at Arjun, determination in her eyes. "We'll crack this," she said softly.

"I know," Arjun replied, flipping the pages of the diary, hoping the answers were buried somewhere within the lines.

16 October's Morning, Kashmir

Shreya entered the room with the four girls, her sharp eyes scanning each of their faces. She pulled out a chair and sat down, her voice calm but piercing. "Which one of you is going to tell me the name of this mission?" The room was filled with silence; none of them dared to speak. Shreya leaned forward slightly, her tone firm. "Your plan has already failed, so there's no point in holding back. But if you decide to help me, I'll let you go."

After a tense pause, Fatima hesitantly broke the silence. "I'm not sure, but, it could be the 'Four-Angle Plan, as I heard those men taking this name"

Shreya immediately grabbed her phone and called Arjun. "Try 'Four-Angle Plan,'" she instructed. Maya quickly typed it into the laptop, and her face lit up as the screen unlocked. "It's correct," she confirmed, already delving into the files.

Meanwhile, Arjun called Vishesh, who has been tailed by Salman. "Is he still following you?" Arjun asked. Vishesh's response was cautious. "I thought he was onto us, but two minutes ago, I saw him take a sharp left and speed off." The phone was on speaker, and Maya looked up at Arjun, her expression worried. "He must have realized his laptop is unlocked. He's likely received a notification."

"What about our location? Is it exposed?" Arjun asked.

Maya checked the settings. "No. Thankfully, this is an old Indian laptop, and for some reason, Salman hasn't changed the default location settings. We're safe for now."

Arjun quickly dialed the building's security guard. "Is Salman at home?"

The guard replied, "Yes, he's in the parking lot right now."

Arjun didn't waste another second. He called his team. "Stay alert. Now is the time to catch him."

Suddenly, Maya froze, her hands clutching her head. Arjun's eyes narrowed with concern. "What's the matter? Did you find something?"

Maya's voice was filled with urgency as she explained. "Salman has engineered a sophisticated triggering mechanism. The bombs will detonate in 10-minute intervals once activated. The countdown is controlled by a central software ".

Arjun frowned, struggling to follow. "Explain it in simpler terms."

Maya took a breath. "Salman planted the bombs in a 2-kilometer radius, right?"

"Correct," Arjun confirmed.

"So, he's written a program that acts as a trigger. Once activated, it will detonate one bomb, then another after 10 minutes, and so on. Each explosion is carefully timed to create chaos. People will flee one site and gather at the next closest site, making them easy targets for the next blast."

Arjun's face turned grim as he pieced it together. "The first bomb will go off at the school. Panic will break out, and the crowd will rush to the nearest open area—the masjid ground, just 750 meters away. Ten minutes later, the second bomb will explode there. From there, the only route out is through the main market, where people will be heading in desperation. In another 10 minutes, the third bomb will detonate. Finally, the sabzi mandi—being the last open space in the area—will be the site of the fourth explosion." His voice grew taut with urgency. "It's a perfect chain of destruction."

Maya's hands hovered over the laptop. "We have limited time to stop this," she said, her voice steady despite the weight of her words. Arjun's eyes burned with determination as he barked into the phone, "Team, this is it. We stop him now, or it's all over."

Arjun's expression turned grave; his eyes fixed on Maya. "Can you do something to stop this?" he asked his voice firm but tinged with urgency.

Maya nodded; her fingers poised over the keyboard. "Yes, I can try to disable the events, but it's going to take some time."

Arjun slipped on his shoes; his resolve unshaken. "You work on breaking the trigger or whatever it takes. I'm going after Salman." Without another word, he grabbed his jacket and left, locking the door behind him.

Mr. Saroha's Apartment

Salman entered the apartment, his demeanor calm and composed. He headed straight to his room when Mrs. Saroha called out from the living room. "Tanay, do you know Shahista?"

His heart skipped a beat, but he turned back with a faint smile. "Yes. Why do you ask?"

"She came by today and took her belongings," Mrs. Saroha replied casually.

Salman forced a polite smile. "Yes, I'm aware," he said and quickly retreated to his room. Locking the door behind him, he crouched down and pulled out a box from under the bed. His smile vanished, replaced by a look of pure shock. The laptop was gone.

Realization hit him like a bolt of lightning. It was Maya. She had found the laptop and uncovered his plan. Panic flared in his chest, but he forced himself to stay composed. He opened his backup laptop, the one he used in the office conference room, and began typing furiously. Lines of code streamed across the screen as he added a layer of security to his trigger system.

Hotel Niagara Inn

Maya sat in front of Salman's laptop, her eyes focused, her fingers moving with practiced precision. She had almost managed to stop the chain of events when the screen abruptly changed. A prompt appeared, and her heart sank.

"It's asking for passwords now," she muttered, her voice laced with frustration. Salman had updated the trigger, and now every event could only be activated or canceled with specific security codes.

The screen displayed a list of cryptic hints:

- Hint 1: "The date that changed everything for me."

- Hint 2: "The bird that sings in a cage."

- Hint 3: "The place where my journey began.

- Hint 4: "A promise I made to the one who betrayed me."

Maya leaned back, her mind racing to decipher the clues. Time was slipping through her fingers, and the weight of the situation bore heavily on her. She whispered to herself, "Come on, think… there has to be a way."

Chapter 12

The Takedown

After realizing that Maya had taken his laptop and diary, Salman knew his time was running out. He just needed to hold on for ten more hours—until 9 AM India time, when the first bomb was set to detonate. Right now, it was 10:30 PM of October 16 in Canada, any moment now, someone would arrive to get him.

Salman opened his suitcase, pulling out a gun. He twisted a silencer onto the barrel, testing its fit before stepping out of his room. In the dimly lit hall, Mrs. Saroha sat watching TV. The sight of the gun made her freeze, her eyes widening in fear.

"Mrs. Saroha," Salman said in a low, measured tone. "There's no need to be afraid. I just need a few hours, so if you cooperate, I will spare your life". Mrs. Saroha swallowed hard and nodded, her lips pressed tightly together. She dared not argue. For four months, she had rented her guest room to him—Tanay Awasthi, or so he had claimed, an old college acquaintance of her nephew from India. But now, with the cold steel of a gun in his hands, she realized she had never truly known the man in her home.

Outside the building, the winter night was quiet. A black SUV was parked discreetly across the street. Inside, Arjun and his team were finalizing their plan. Their mission was clear: capture Salman alive without drawing attention. Any commotion could alert Canadian police and authorities, complicating diplomatic ties.

Arjun adjusted the earpiece in his ear. "Team, remember—no firearms unless absolutely necessary. We have the master key, so we take him quietly. Mrs. Saroha's safety is our priority. Move in."

Two officers slipped through the back entrance; their footsteps muffled against the cold floor. They climbed the staircase swiftly and silently. Arjun and another officer approached the front.

Arjun knocked lightly on the door. "Maintenance," the other officer called out in a calm voice.

Inside, Salman tensed. He grabbed Mrs. Saroha and pulled her toward the coat closet near the entrance, pressing the barrel of his gun against her side. "Stay quiet," he ordered.

Arjun knocked again, louder this time. "Ma'am, we need to check for a water leak. The family downstairs filed an urgent complaint."

At Arjun's signal, the fellow officer slid the master key into the lock and turned it. The door burst open. Arjun stepped inside with controlled precision—just as Salman had expected.

The moment they crossed the threshold, Salman struck. He fired, the silencer muffling the gunshot as the second officer collapsed. Arjun spun around, gun raised, but Salman was already behind Mrs. Saroha, using her as a human shield.

"Drop your gun," Salman commanded, his voice steady. "Now. Slide it over."

Arjun hesitated, his jaw tightening. But with his fellow officer dead and Mrs. Saroha trembling under Salman's grip and any commotion that could create panic amongst the other families living on the floor, he had no choice. Slowly, he lowered his weapon and kicked it across the floor.

Salman smirked. "Good. Now move."

The game had shifted in his favor.

Hotel Niagara Inn

Maya flipped through Salman's diary, her hands trembling as she searched for answers. Panic clawed at her chest. Her eyes kept darting to the door, waiting—hoping—for Arjun to return. But time was slipping away, and she couldn't afford to waste another second.

She took a deep breath, forcing herself to focus. With a swift motion, she tied her hair into a ponytail, as if physically bracing herself for the task ahead. "Okay, there's no point in waiting for Arjun," she muttered under her breath. "Let's find the answers. We can't fail without trying."

Steeling her nerves, she turned her attention back to the screen and began reading Hint 1: "**The date that changed everything for me.**" She read each page carefully from Salman's diary. The entries were from Salman's teenage years. One passage made her pause: "I'll never forgive them. The army. They knew. They could have saved my parents, but they didn't. because they were locals, not tourists. Our lives meant nothing to them." a flood that swept through his hometown, and he lost both his parents to the flood.

Determined to find a clue, she opened her laptop and searched for records of floods in Kashmir over the past 15 years. The articles flashed on the screen, and she scrolled quickly, her breath quickening as her eyes skimmed the headlines. Then she saw it: "Kashmir Floods: 17th October

2008—Devastation Unfolds." Her heart skipped a beat. That date explained why Salman had chosen October 17th. Not only because it's the inauguration date of the school but it was the day that changed everything for him.

Her fingers hovered over the keyboard. She glanced at the screen of the laptop in front of her, the password still unknown. Maya whispered a prayer: "Hey Durga Ma, please help me." Taking a deep breath, she typed 17-10- 2008 and hit enter. After ten agonizing seconds, Maya slowly opened her eyes, her heart pounding. She had squeezed them shut out of fear while pressing enter, expecting for a failure—but now, the screen in front of her had changed. She could access the code.

A sharp breath of relief escaped her lips. There was no time to waste. Her fingers flew across the keyboard, typing frantically to cancel the event. Each second felt like an eternity. Then, finally, a message flashed across the screen:

"Successful."

Maya exhaled, her hands trembling. She had done it.

Kashmir, 17th October, 3:30 AM

Back at the base, tension filled the air as Colonel Ahlawat sat with Shreya and the rest of the team. They were reviewing the security plan for the upcoming event when Yuvraj burst into the room.

"Sir, we've located the bombs," he announced, his voice laced with urgency. "But the bomb squad says they can't deactivate them. They're programmed, time-sensitive devices with no wires to cut. We'll have to rely on Arjun and Maya to disable them."

Colonel Ahlawat immediately picked up the phone, dialing Arjun.

"Why isn't he answering?" he muttered, his voice tight with concern. Something felt off. His instincts, sharpened by years in the field, told him this was more than just a delayed response. Without wasting another second, he called one of the officers from Arjun's team.

"What's the update? Where is Arjun?"

The officer responded promptly; his voice steady but laced with tension. "Sir, Arjun is inside Mrs. Saroha's apartment, he got captured before he was captured, he had turned on his smartwatch's emergency distress signal, and we are already tracking his movements. with his SOS we knew something was wrong when no response came. We're on high alert, waiting outside."

Colonel Ahlawat's grip tightened around the phone. "Stay there until Arjun signals you. No one moves without his command."

Suddenly, Yuvraj rushed into the room, breathless. "Sir—the first bomb... it stopped ticking!"

Colonel Ahlawat's head snapped up. His brows furrowed for a brief moment before Shreya, sitting nearby, let out a relieved smile.

"Must be Maya in action," she said confidently.

Hotel Niagara Inn

Maya exhaled deeply, the tension in her shoulders easing slightly. The weight of what she had just accomplished settled in—she had defused the first bomb. She took a sip of water, her eyes flickering to the door, half-expecting Arjun to walk in any moment. But she forced herself to refocus. There was still more to do.

She turned back to the laptop screen, her fingers hovering over the keys as she read the next clue:

"Hint 2: The bird that sings in a cage."

The words hung in the air, circling her thoughts. She repeated them under her breath, trying to unravel their meaning.

Maya sat cross-legged on the bed; her brow furrowed in concentration. She murmured to herself, thinking aloud. "Reading Salman's diary, I can tell he's deeply emotional, scarred. Losing his parents so young and being misguided shaped him… but there's nothing about a bird or any pet."

She scanned the room absentmindedly until her gaze landed on a painting on the wall. It showed a girl sitting behind a window, her expression somber. Above her head, a swarm of butterflies fluttered, as if the artist was trying to depict her longing to escape.

Maya straightened. The bird isn't literal—it's symbolic. Something trapped. Something Salman had been yearning for.

And then, it hit her. A memory from the office team lunch flashed in her mind. The HR had organized a game where everyone had to pick a chit and answer a personal question. She remembered the chit Salman, then known as Tanay—had drawn:

"What do you think is better here in Canada than in your own country?"

She could still hear his voice in her head, the way he had laughed casually as he answered:

"I feel more freedom here. Back home, I always felt like I was trapped in a cage."

Maya had disliked his response at the time but hadn't thought much of it. Now, the pieces clicked together.

Her eyes widened. "Freedom," she whispered. "The bird isn't a bird—it's freedom."

Her fingers trembled as she typed "freedom" into the password field.

Before pressing enter, she closed her eyes. "Durga Ma, please help me," she murmured.

Then, she hit enter, she smiled ii confidence as she could now access the second code too to stop the second event to defuse the second bomb.

Kashmir 5 AM

Colonel Ahlawat and his team stood over the two captured militants, their expressions cold and unyielding. These are the men Salman had been communicating with—the ones responsible for planting the bombs. But despite the intense questioning, even after hours of merciless interrogation, their answer remained the same.

"Our role was just to plant the bombs. We know nothing else."

Frustration simmered in the room, but Colonel Ahlawat didn't let it show. He knew fear could break a man, but conviction could make him resist even the worst pain. He was about to order another round of questioning when the door opened.

Shreya stepped in, her voice calm but urgent. "Sir, good news. The second one's done too."

Colonel Ahlawat controlled his expression, but the weight on his shoulders lightened slightly. Yet, the relief was short-lived—there was still no word from Arjun.

He clenched his jaw. Where the hell is he?

Mrs. Saroha's Apartment

The room was dimly lit, the tension thick like a storm waiting to break. Arjun sat bound to the dining chairs, ropes digging into his wrists and Mrs.Saroha was also sitting scared on a chair a few feet away from Arjun, she was not tied, for her Salman was sure this old lady was not going to do anything, Across from them, Salman sat with his gun casually pointed at Mrs. Saroha, his finger resting on the trigger. He leaned forward slightly, eyes gleaming with amusement.

"So," Salman began, his voice mockingly polite. "You're not a dentist, are you?"

Arjun smirked but didn't reply.

Salman slammed his palm against the table, the sound echoing through the silent room. "How did you find me?"

Arjun met his gaze, unshaken. "Correct. I'm not a dentist," he said coolly. "And I found you through the little slips you were passing from the coaching center to the café—using innocent girls as couriers."

Salman's lips curled into a smirk. "Oh… Indian Army." He chuckled darkly, shaking his head. "So, you came all the way here to stop me? And you thought—with Maya's help—you could actually pull it off?"

Arjun's eyes narrowed. Salman's confidence sent a chill down his spine. There was something he wasn't saying but was too confident about.

Salman suddenly leaned forward, his voice dropping to a whisper. "She's smart, I'll give her that. She probably managed to break in and stop the trigger."

"But…" Salman let the word hang, savoring the moment.

Arjun's stomach dropped. "But what?" he demanded.

Salman leaned even closer, his voice dripping with triumph. "I added security questions. Not Maya or anyone can break through them." He leaned back with a satisfied sigh. "My plan is failure-proof now. It's just a matter of a few more hours."

Arjun's hands clenched into fists, his jaw tightening. Damn it. He had underestimated Salman. He had left in such a hurry, he hadn't even realized—Maya had no phone to contact anyone. At that moment Arjun felt helpless and was constantly looking for a way to reverse the current scene.

Hotel Niagara Inn

Maya is now looking at **Hint 3: "The place where my journey began"**.

she was unsure but she remembered Arjun telling her about Salman tutoring at the coaching center and the girls," What's the name of the coaching center? Come on Maya just think "She tried hard to recall the name, Aftab Coaching Center." Her eyes widened with excitement.

She quickly grabbed the laptop to enter this name but she realized that the password couldn't be this long the character length looks longer.

Without wasting any single moment she picked up the diary again, flipping through the pages until she stopped at an entry about the day Salman got his job at the coaching center. Her eyes scanned the words until she noticed something. "Every time Salman mentions the coaching center, he uses an Urdu phrase—Zehni Urooj."

"What does that mean?" she wondered.

She quickly searched the meaning "It means 'Mental Elevation,' a metaphor for intellectual growth."

Snapping her fingers, she claimed confidently, "That's it, it should be Zehni Urooj."

Maya entered the word into the laptop, her fingers trembling once again. "Please help me, Durga Ma," she murmured before hitting enter.

Kashmir 7 AM

Shreya's voice came through, calm yet relieved. "Three down Sir"

Col Ahlawat who was still worried as it was already 7 AM no news from Arjun, this message from Shreya gave him a belief that we can still stop this.

He called the officers from Arjun's team again" Any movement ?", "Negative Sir" the officer replied, Col

Ahlawat instructed them to get inside the building if there was no movement in the next 30 minutes as we are running short on time we still have one more bomb to defuse.

Mrs. Saroha's Apartment

The room was thick with tension, the only sounds coming from the occasional crackle of the heater and the ticking of the wall clock. Arjun sat bound to the dining chair, his hands tightly secured behind him. Mrs. Saroha sat a few feet away, her face pale with fear.

Salman paced in front of them, the gun in his hand swinging lazily at his side. He seemed very confident, "two more hours," Salman mused, checking his watch. And laughed like a maniac.

Arjun remained calm; his expression unreadable. He knew brute force wouldn't get him out of this—not yet. He had to break Salman first.

"You sound pretty sure of yourself," Arjun said, his voice laced with doubt.

Salman's eyes flickered toward him. "I am."

Arjun tilted his head slightly. "Are you? Because I was just thinking... Maya's a lot smarter than you gave her credit for."

Salman scoffed. "She may be smart, but she can't break through my security questions. I made sure of that."

Arjun nodded slowly, studying him. "Hmm what if you overlooked something? What if Maya's already cracked your security questions? Did you forget she had your diary?"

Salman's smirk faltered slightly.

Arjun leaned in, his voice dropping to a conspiratorial whisper. "See, that's the thing about overconfidence, Salman. It blinds you. Maybe Maya already broke in. Maybe she's watching the countdown right now, laughing at how easy it was to override your so-called failproof plan."

A muscle twitched in Salman's jaw. "You're bluffing."

Arjun smiled. "Am I?" He shrugged. "You could just sit here and assume you're right. But what if you're wrong? What if the system is already compromised?

Salman hesitated. His grip on the gun tightened slightly. Then, as if to reassure himself, he strode toward the laptop on the kitchen counter.

That was the opening Arjun needed.

He subtly adjusted his weight, shifting the chair's balance ever so slightly. As soon as Salman leaned over to type in his credentials, Arjun threw himself backward with full force. The chair tipped over, crashing against the floor with a deafening BANG!

This was to signal is team waiting outside.

"NOW!" Arjun shouted.

Mrs. Saroha, already gripping the burning candle placed on the dining table, as Arjun had subtly signaled earlier, hurled it straight at Salman's face. The hot wax splattered across his cheek, and he let out a pained roar, stumbling backward.

The two officers were already inside the apartment, aiming their guns at Salman.

Mrs. Saroha, trembling but determined, untied Arjun's arms. He wasted no time. In a flash, he ripped the rest of the rope off and launched at Salman. Before the militant could recover, Arjun grabbed him by the collar and slammed him face-first against the table.

Salman groaned, trying to fight back, but Arjun twisted his arm behind his back, locking him in place.

"You underestimated the wrong people," Arjun growled, grabbing the gun from the floor and pressing it against Salman's temple. "Game over."

Arjun tightened his grip on Salman's collar and dialed Colonel Ahlawat.

"We got Salman," Arjun reported, his breath steady despite the adrenaline still coursing through his veins.

Colonel Ahlawat's voice came through, calm but firm. "Great. Just make sure to keep him alive and get him out quietly. We might need him—there's still one bomb left to be defused, and we only have 60 minutes now."

Arjun's brows furrowed. "Wait... so Maya already defused three?"

"Yes," Ahlawat confirmed. "She did it. Try to contact her and see how she's progressing on the fourth."

Arjun's jaw clenched. "Sir, Maya doesn't have a phone with her right now. She's handling everything on her own."

A beat of silence. Then Ahlawat exhaled sharply. "That girl is a damn miracle."

Hotel Niagara Inn

Maya's eyes scanned the laptop screen, the countdown ticking dangerously low.

Hint 4: "A promise I made to the one who betrayed me."

Her mind was blank. No clues, no instincts—just mounting pressure. 45 minutes left.

She flipped through Salman's diary again, fingers trembling. Every page is blurred together. She took a deep breath, a sip of water, and forced herself to focus.

"Okay, think. He lost his parents. He was vulnerable. He was misled into believing Kashmir was caged. He thinks the Indian Army is the enemy. Is the password 'Indian Army'?"

No. That didn't fit the betrayal part.

Maya's pulse quickened. She had studied Salman's psychology through his writings. He started this mission after the repeal of Article 370. That was his turning point. That was when his hate deepened.

Her breath hitched. "The government."

Her fingers hovered over the keyboard. "He believes that the Indian Government betrayed Kashmir, played smart, and lifted 370. That has to be it."

20 minutes left

She closed her eyes. "Please, Durga Ma, let this be right."

She typed: Indian Government.

Her finger hovered over the Enter key. Then—she pressed it.

Kashmir - 8:45 AM

Yuvraj rushed into the command center. "Sir, the function has already started. The fourth bomb is set to explode near Subzi Mandi. We've evacuated most of the area, but if this one goes off, the impact radius is short enough to cause massive damage."

Colonel Ahlawat's hands curled into fists. He shut his eyes, preparing to issue the final evacuation orders.

Then—Shreya burst into the room, breathless.

"Sir! Maya did it! All four bombs are defused!"

For a second, silence. Then relief crashed over them like a wave.

Colonel Ahlawat's face broke into a rare smile. "She did it."

He immediately called Arjun. "What's the update?"

Arjun, who was now getting into the extraction vehicle with Salman, responded, "Sir, we got him out."

Ahlawat interrupted, "Great job, both of you. Maya defused all four bombs."

Arjun's shoulders slumped with relief. A small, proud smile tugged at his lips. "That's great news, sir. I'll visit her now."

But Colonel Ahlawat's tone turned serious. "No, Arjun. I've already made arrangements for your departure. Head to the airport now. Someone else will collect the evidence from Maya."

Arjun froze. "Sir… but—"

"That's an order."

The line went dead.

Arjun swallowed the lump in his throat. His heart ached. He should have checked if she had a phone before leaving. He should have called her. He should have told her how proud he was. How much he… loved her.

But duty came first.

He inhaled sharply, forcing his emotions down.

"On my way, sir."

She immediately called Vishesh" Go pick Maya and make sure she is safely dropped to her apartment

I am sending one of my men too to pick up evidence from Maya".

Hotel Niagara Inn

Maya shut the laptop lid the moment she saw the success message flash across the screen. Her heart pounded with exhilaration—she had done it. The fourth bomb was stopped.

Overwhelmed with relief, she twirled on the spot, whispering, "Thank you, Durga Maa." Her hands folded in silent gratitude.

But her joy wasn't just for the mission. She was waiting—any minute now, Arjun would burst through that door. She could already picture it: the warmth of his embrace, the words she had been holding back for so long finally slipping from her lips.

The door creaked open.

Maya's heart leaped as she turned, smiling brightly—

Only for her face to fall.

It wasn't Arjun. It was Dr. Vishesh.

His expression was hesitant as he greeted her, "Hi, Maya."

Her throat ran dry. "Dr. Vishesh… where is Arjun?"

Vishesh sighed. "He got orders. He left for the airport. He's heading back to Kashmir."

The room spun. Her breath hitched, and for a moment, she couldn't move.

Before she could react, another officer entered. "Ma'am, I need the laptop and the diary."

Maya's gaze flickered to Vishesh, searching for confirmation.

"Arjun sent him," Vishesh assured her softly. "He's from the team. It's fine."

Numbly, Maya picked up the laptop and diary, but as she held them out, her fingers clenched around the diary for a moment longer. She inhaled shakily, then pulled a piece of paper from the table, scribbled a few words, and slipped it inside before handing everything over.

Vishesh watched her carefully. "Maya…"

She blinked, swallowing the lump in her throat. "Do you have my phone?"

He nodded, retrieving it from his pocket and placing it in her palm. She dialed Arjun's number instantly.

The automated voice response cut through the silence— "The number you are trying to reach is switched off."

Vishesh's voice was gentle. "Get ready, Maya. I'll drop you home. It's over. Everything will be back to normal now."

Maya smiled, but it was faded, empty.

Nothing would ever be normal again.

Final Chapter

Unfinished Words, Unspoken Feelings

The car came to a gentle stop. Vishesh turned to Maya, his voice soft. "Maya, we've reached."

She stirred, her eyes fluttering open. "Hmm?" For a moment, she had forgotten where she was. Then reality sank in.

It was over.

She sat up, rubbing her eyes. "Thank you, Vishesh."

As she reached for the door, his voice stopped her. "Maya, listen… you can't mention this mission to anyone. I repeat, no one."

Maya met his gaze, the weight of his words sinking in. She nodded, stepping out without another word.

The doorbell rang.

Smriti flung the door open, her face lighting up. "Mimi! Finally, you're back after three days!"

Maya barely had time to step inside before Smriti bombarded her with questions—Where were you? Why was your phone off? Do you know how worried I was?

But the words faded into background noise.

Her mind was elsewhere. Her fingers kept scrolling through her phone. No messages. No calls. Nothing.

She sighed. "Sim, can we talk later? I'm really tired. I just need some rest."

Smriti frowned, noticing her dull expression, but nodded. "Okay... but we'll talk later, alright?"

Maya gave a faint smile and walked to her room, shutting the door behind her.

She leaned against it, staring at her phone screen one last time. Still nothing.

Kashmir

At the army base, cheers filled the air. The mission was a success.

Colonel Ahlawat stood before the team, his chest swelling with pride. "Congratulations, everyone. You've done an exceptional job today."

Arjun nodded respectfully. "Sir, Maya played a major role in our success."

Shreya grinned. "Oh yes! Arjun, call her! Let's thank her properly."

But before Arjun could reach for his phone, Colonel Ahlawat's voice cut through the air.

"Nobody is calling or mentioning Maya's name." His expression was serious. "For her own safety, she must remain anonymous. She is still in Canada. Her name should stay confidential."

A lump formed in Arjun's throat. He couldn't even thank her?

Colonel Ahlawat turned to him. "Did you submit all the evidence?"

Arjun straightened. "Yes, Sir."

The Colonel's gaze didn't waver. "Good. Now, hand over your phone too."

Arjun's heart clenched.

The Colonel continued, "Your visit to Canada wasn't documented. No loose ends, Arjun. We can't take any risks."

Arjun hesitated. His phone was the only bridge between him and Maya. The only way to tell her how proud he was.

With a heavy heart, he handed over the phone.

10 Days Later, Maya's Apartment

Smriti walked into the apartment and saw Maya typing on her laptop.

"Hi Maya, still working?"

Maya didn't look up, her eyes fixed on the screen. "Not really. I'm applying for leave."

Smriti frowned. "Leave? So suddenly? Is everything okay?"

Maya finally lifted her gaze. "Yes, just going home for a few days. Dad's been calling me, and it's been two years since I left India."

Smriti rushed to her side, scanning her face carefully. "Maya, look at me. Just tell me what's wrong. You're usually quiet, but this time… this silence feels different. It feels like a disappointment." She paused. "Is it that dentist? Did he break your heart? Just tell me."

Maya smiled faintly. "No, nothing like that. Vishesh and I are just friends, nothing more."

Smriti gave her a skeptical look. "Really? Because that day, he was claiming you were his girlfriend."

Maya chuckled. "You know how he is, always joking around. He must've been messing with you."

Smriti sighed. "When are you leaving?"

"Tomorrow afternoon," Maya replied, closing her laptop. "Now I have to pack." She walked off, leaving Smriti staring after her.

The Smile Dental Clinic

The next morning, Vishesh was mid-conversation with a patient when his phone rang. A number he didn't recognize. He ignored it.

A text popped up: "Hi buddy, it's me. Pick up the call."

The phone rang again. Vishesh sighed and answered. "Finally, you got time?" he said sarcastically.

Arjun's laugh came through the line. "Sorry, bro. Things got a little crazy. One of my teammates got shot that day, and you know, formalities took time. Just bought a new phone today."

Vishesh narrowed his eyes. "What happened to your old phone?"

Arjun ignored the question. "How's Maya? Did you drop her off safely that night? Did she say anything? How was she looking? Did you tell her I was sorry for not coming?"

Vishesh groaned. "So many questions. Yes, I dropped her safely. She looked disappointed. And yes, I told her you had to leave." He paused. "As for the rest, call her yourself."

Arjun exhaled. "Send me her number. I'm dying to talk to her."

Maya's Apartment – Departure Day

It was nearly 10 AM, and Maya was in a rush to leave for the airport. Her phone was pressed to her ear as she explained the location to her cab driver, who was waiting at the wrong building.

Just as she stepped out of the apartment, her phone rang—an unknown number.

She hesitated but before she could answer, the cab honked. Prioritizing her ride, she declined the call and hurried into the car.

Five minutes into the ride, Smriti called. Maya answered, keeping the phone busy.

At the same time, Arjun called. Once, twice, thrice. Each time, the call went to waiting.

Maya sighed, glancing at her phone, "Some unknown number keeps calling."

Smriti shrugged. "Must be spam. Ignore it."

Arjun tried again after two hours. By then, Maya's phone was switched off.

She had boarded her flight.

Arjun stared at his phone, defeated. Still, he sent a message.

"Hi Maya, it's me, Arjun. Please call when you can."

But the message wouldn't deliver.

Frustrated, he called Vishesh again. "Can you check on Maya? Her phone is off."

Vishesh smirked. "Sure, bro. Anything for your love."

Maya's Apartment – Later That Day

Smriti opened the door, surprised to see Vishesh standing there, phone in hand.

"Hi, Dr. Vishesh. How are you?" she asked.

Vishesh smiled. "I'm great as always. Can you call Maya, please?"

Smriti raised an eyebrow. "Oh? So that day you were bluffing about Maya being your girlfriend?"

Vishesh frowned. "What?"

Smriti sighed dramatically. "If she's your girlfriend, then why don't you know she left for India?"

Vishesh straightened. "She left?"

"Yes, this afternoon. She must be on the flight already."

His expression shifted. He lifted his phone back to his ear. "Bro, she left."

Vishesh's voice was tense. "Did you send her your number?"

"Yes, but it was a text message and she won't get the message until she is back in the network and that will be when she turns her phone on in Canada. If she stays in India for a while... she won't even know I tried."

Silence.

Then, a quiet click.

Arjun had hung up.

After 2 weeks, Kashmir

Arjun and the team were eating lunch and suddenly Shreya came running "Arjun sir," Arjun stood up and asked in a tense voice "What happened Shreya?" She handed over a note. to Arjun, he asked "What's this, Shreya responded "I was just making a file on Salman's case so I visited to see the evidence again, I found this one in Salman's diary.

Arjun opened the note it was an address:

"Mr. Ashok Majumdar

House No. 105 Street no.3

Defense Colony, New Delhi"

Shreya was suspicious "Whose address is this"? A smile cracked on Arjun's face and ran to the officer whom he sent to collect the diary from Maya, "Did Maya give this note to you"? He responded, "Oh yes sir, she wrote a note and hid it in this diary I forgot to mention that before sir". Arjun was jumping in happiness and said "She is still waiting for me".

2 Days later, Delhi

The doorbell rang.

Maya opened the door and froze. Her heart, which had spent weeks convincing itself to move on, betrayed her in that single moment.

She took a deep breath, setting down her book. It had been days of waiting, hoping, and finally giving up. She told herself that if he really wanted to come, he would have.

But now, standing on the other side of that door… was him.

"Arjun".

With slightly trembling hands, she unlocked the door. As it creaked open, her breath hitched.

There he was.

Wearing his usual dark jacket over a plain T-shirt. His eyes—those deep, intense eyes—searched hers, desperate, almost pleading.

"You're late," Maya whispered, gripping the door frame.

Arjun exhaled heavily, his throat tightening at the sight of her. He had imagined this moment a hundred times during his journey, but nothing prepared him for the way she looked at him—hurt, yet still undeniably his.

"I know," he admitted, his voice hoarse. "I got your note too late. When I was able to contact you, I did Maya I promise I did, but you were already gone."

Maya clenched her jaw, her anger bubbling up again. "I waited, Arjun. For days. Do you have any idea what that felt like? After everything… after risking my life to help you, after—" she stopped, swallowing hard, unwilling to let the tears win. "You just left."

Arjun took a step closer. "I didn't have a choice, Maya."

Arjun reached into his pocket and pulled out a folded piece of paper—her note. It was worn from being held too many times. "You wrote this for me, Maya. Do you really think I wouldn't have come if I had seen it sooner?"

Maya looked away, blinking back tears. "It doesn't matter anymore."

"It does," he insisted. "Because I love you."

Maya's breath caught.

Arjun stepped even closer now, closing the space between them. "I don't care how long it took me to get here. I don't care if you yell at me if you slam the door in my face. But don't tell me it doesn't matter, because, for me, you are the only thing that does."

Maya looked up at him, her resolve breaking. "You hurt me, Arjun."

His fingers brushed against hers. "And I'll spend my whole life making it up to you… if you let me."

A tear slipped down her cheek. "You're impossible."

Arjun smiled slightly. "But you love me anyway."

Maya let out a shaky breath. "Yes. I do."

A slow, relieved smile spread across his face before he pulled her into his arms. Maya melted into him, feeling his heartbeat against hers, feeling every second of pain, longing, and love that led them to this moment.

Maya looked into Arjun's eyes, searching for the answer her heart already knew. "Are we soulmates or partners?" she asked softly.

Arjun smiled, gently tucking a strand of hair behind her ear before pressing a kiss to her forehead. "We are soulmates, but as you said that day—if we're sure who our soulmate is, then why can't we make them our partner?" He took her hands in his, his voice steady yet filled with emotion. "So, Maya, you are my soulmate, and I want to make you, my partner. Will you be my partner?"

Maya felt a warmth spread through her chest, her lips curving into a teasing smile. "Yes… but before that, you owe me a dinner. Remember? Maya 2, Vishesh—sorry, sorry—Arjun 0."

Arjun laughed, shaking his head in surrender. "Fine, I accept defeat."

They both burst into laughter, their hearts lighter than they had been in a long time. In that moment, there were no more distances, no more missed calls, no more waiting. Just the two of them, together—soulmates, partners, and finally, home.

©volatile_ Nucleus

(Anju Singh)